Fire and Ice

The Vampire Romance Writer

Fire and Ice

ISBN 9781071240083

Chapter 1

Total Darkness enveloped her, the sound of the
howling wind all but drowned out the faint cries of
Mommy! Mommy! Dillon tried to run as fast as she
could; not being able to see where she was going was
hindering her effort.

Dillon ran toward the voice that she knew to be her
son, her dead son! Where was he? Where was he? As
she ran down the long hall, Dillon heard what she
thought sounded like heavy raindrops as she
approaches the windows ahead, she can see that it was
storming out. The hallway was almost in total darkness
except for the occasional lighting strike but Dillon
continues he is calling her mommy! Mommy!

The Vampire Romance Writer

I am here, you must come, mommy! Mommy! Dillon continues to run faster and faster toward his voice. Mommy! Mommy! Come, as Dillon runs, she can feel the cold wet floor under her bare feet. Rain! Rain was getting in; the walls were gone in one corner on the house gone, but how? It seems to have been blown off, mommy! His voice was fading it seemed to be getting further away the faster she ran in his direction. Mommy.... Lightning strikes again suddenly she sits upright in bed to a bright room all alone.

It was the same type of dream they always contained wind and rain. Why were her dreams that way? Making her feel as if it she was close to tears giving her a feeling of sadness when she woke. Well, she shoved the dream to the back of her mind. It was her day off and she was going to relax.

It was early Dillon had always been an early riser and today was no different. Dillon got up and showered

The Vampire Romance Writer

and dressed for the day she had some errands to run, she was to have dinner with her best friend that evening, and then it would be back to work the next day.

Dillon still had over a week before her vacation and if she kept having those dreams, the week could not pass fast enough. Maybe getting away for a while would help her relax and get rid of those dreams she thought.

The feeling of deep sadness lingered as Dillon left for the restaurant that evening but another sensation had joined the sadness, the feeling of someone watching her!

As she pulled into the parking lot Dillon noticed someone in the shadows of the building next to the restaurant just out of sight to most who passed by.

Dillon felt as though they were watching her, waiting for her. The person did not move any closer and made no attempt to say nothing to her. Dillon continued to the restaurant she could still feel eyes upon her.

5

The Vampire Romance Writer

Dillon could see his silhouette out of the corner of her eye but as she was entering the door to the restaurant, she turned to get a closer look, but he was gone, gone in an instant.

Dillon walked on into the restaurant where Sarah her friend of ten years was waiting for her. Hi Dillon, over here Sarah called.

Dillon walked over and sat down; she noticed that Sarah had already ordered her a coke.

Sarah was her closest friend; Dillon could tell her anything and Sarah would always give her an honest answer even if it were not what she wanted to hear.

Tonight, though Dillon decided not to say anything about the man in the shadows and of her feeling of being watched, she did not want Sarah to get worried, as they would be going on vacation together, she wanted everything to go smoothly.

The Vampire Romance Writer

This was her first vacation without her children, well they were not children anymore with her youngest in her first year of college and her other two off on their own this vacation would most certainly be different.

So how is everything going at work? "Sarah asks", things were busy as usual the hospital was busy this time of year it seemed every year the snowbirds came down to Florida and they would either work themselves into a heart attack or fall and break something, so the hospital was always full this time of year. How is your part-time retirement?

Sarah was a nurse the same as Dillon, but Sarah was a little over twenty years older than Dillon, but you could not tell it by her actions or by the way she looked Sarah still looked as if she was in her forties and still had an active social life.

Sarah continued work a few days a month as a hospice nurse.

The Vampire Romance Writer

They had so much in common despite their age difference it was as if they were twins separated not at birth but at some unknown point in time.

Dillon worked twelve-hour shifts, three days a week at one of the local hospitals and that left her with a lot of time on her hands. Dillon and Sarah would hang out whenever Sarah was in town or when Dillon could get down south to visit her.

Even though Sarah was, much older Dillon the age difference was never a problem Dillon always seems to connect with people much older than her. So, are you ready for our two weeks in Colorado Dillon?

Well as long as you don't try to get me on any slopes. Because that's not why I want to go there said Dillon, I am looking forward to just sitting by a window and a roaring fire, relaxing reading a good book, and just enjoying the snowy scenery. Tell me about the cabin you have booked for us.

8

The Vampire Romance Writer

While Dillon was telling Sarah all about the cabin, Dillon continued to have the feeling of being watched but as she scanned the restaurant, she saw no one.

The feeling continued as they left the restaurant. Still, Dillon did not voice her feelings to Sarah, no use worrying her about her strange feeling, as she was sure that had to be the lingering effects of last night's dream.

I'll call you later to see if you made home ok, Dillon said as Sarah lived four hours away and would stay a few days up here to visit her son and daughter as often as she could but tonight Sarah would be driving back home to South Florida. Talk to you later Sarah said as she was pulling away.

Dillon drove back to her apartment and was glad to be home. Even though she did not see anyone, she still could not shake the feeling of being watched.

Dillon spent the rest of the evening finalizing their vacation plans eventually dozing off at her computer.

The Vampire Romance Writer

It was dark and raining she could hear the wind outside, there was no lighting but there was light but from where was it coming?

There was just enough to light for her to recognize that she was back at the house with the corner blown off. This time she did not hear the boy calling her, but she did hear someone she could not tell what they were saying.

Dillon started walking down the long hall again with the wind and rain fiercely blowing just outside the window. Dillon was getting closer to the voice. However, the light seemed to fade, as Dillon got closer to the source.

As Dillon neared the end of the long hall with the blown off corner, she noticed that this time someone stood off in the shadows ahead. A man dressed in all black, his face was shielded by the darkness, his mouth was all that she could make out he seemed to

The Vampire Romance Writer

be speaking very fast. There was no sound coming from the dark stranger's lips.

Dillon could tell he was desperately trying to speak to her. Suddenly Dillon was filled with fear and she knew that she needed to get as far away from him as possible. As Dillon started to run, she heard a blood-curdling scream of Noooo!!!

When she woke up, she was still at her desk feeling this time not sadness but fear. Fear so intense that she felt her heart was ready to free itself from her chest. Dillon sat there for a few minutes letting her heart slow down somewhat close too normal.

As Dillon sat there, looking out her window trying to compose herself she noticed that it was just starting to get dark out.

The darkness combined with the fear that lingered from her dream and the earlier feeling that someone was watching her gave her the feeling of impending doom.

11

The Vampire Romance Writer

Chapter 2

Dillon got up, rubbed her hands through her long strawberry blond hair, and went to run her a hot bath, as her bath was running, she checked all her windows and doors.

After ensuring that were secure Dillon checked her cell there were no messages, she walked to her computer intent on checking her e-mail but decided not to just being at her computer got her to thinking about her dream again.

While she waited for her bath to fill Dillon went to the kitchen put a cup of water in the microwave, her dream surfacing again as she waited for the microwave to beep signaling that her water was ready.

Finally, the familiar beeping sound broke into her thoughts. Dillon made her a cup of chamomile tea walked back to her bath adding bath salts before

12

undressing and stepping into the hot water. The heat from the water made all the muscles in her body relax.

Dillon remained there for a long time letting the tension and the dream be washed away by the hot water.

Sitting in her tub Dillon thought at least here she felt lucky that there were no windows in her bathroom in there she did not feel any eyes upon her. After her bath she pulled on her pajamas and got into bed, 5 am would come too soon.

Dillon snuggled under the covers and was fast asleep. Dillon was shivering the cold seemed to be creeping in all around her, once again she was walking down the long hall, this time she did not see anyone, but she heard a man saying come! Come! Come to me, she quickly turned away Dillon had a feeling that she needed run, run away from him, she had the feeling that if she went to him, she would be in grave danger.

As she turned to run, she heard him, he screamed again Noooooo! Then alarms starting sounding all around her. Dillon woke up to her alarm clock ringing and flashing 5 am.

Outside her window, he was watching her, he knew he did not have long before dawn, but he had to stay as long as he could, she mesmerized him.

He had not moved from that spot all night he sat there just watching and wondering why he has not sensed her before. Wondering what to do next, he had never been attracted to a woman like this before.

He had a soul burning feeling of total devastation when he thought of leaving her side. He knew that he would have to leave her the sun would be up soon, and he needed to think and to try to figure out what to do next.

He knew if he went to her now he would not be able to control himself he would not be able to stop at the

14

sexual desire his body longed for he would want more, and he could not allow himself to lose control he would not let that happen not to her.

He was not going to lose something that he thought that he would never have. In addition, to act carelessly now would be the greatest mistake he would ever make.

Not in all the years that he has lived on this earth had, he had these kinds of feelings before for any woman and he had spent far too many a lonely year searching to no avail.

He had to wait, seek answers, answers to questions that were tearing him apart, but he would have to leave her for the moment and he was scared to death that in doing so he would lose her and would not be able to find her again.

He heard her alarm sound, which brought him back to the present he watched as she got out of bed and walked to her closet to dress. He continued to watch as she slid off her pajama's exposing her flawless

15

The Vampire Romance Writer

porcelain skin, not a blemish on it except for her freckles which only made her that more beautiful.

He could smell her scent from where he was clean, fresh like the smell of the ocean; this only increased his desire for her.

He continued to watch as she walked to the window as if she was looking for someone, like she knew he was watching, but he had placed himself where she could not see him, but where he could see her clearly, he knew that if he stayed there any longer he would not be able to control himself.

The monster inside would take total control and would consume her in more ways than one.

He could not take the torture he had to get away and in an instant, he was gone.

He got into his car and he drove, drove so fast the landscape was a blur he had to distance himself from her had to find release and fulfillment and he had to

16

The Vampire Romance Writer

do before he lost control and turned around and take what he needed from her and he knew he would not stop until she was lifeless.

He was close to his hunting ground now, as he was slowing down, he sensed his prey walking down the dark long lamp-lit street, he pulled up to her reached across the seat and opened the passenger door she got in without a word and they speed off pulling up to a rundown hotel.

He parked next to the last room in the back and used an all-access keycard he had kept for times like this and led her into the room.

No sooner had the door shut that he took her, and she realized that this was not going to end well, she started to protest but that did no good he was strong, stronger than anyone she had ever encountered it was as if he was a wild animal and she was his first meal in weeks.

He was enraged to the point of no return he had satisfied his sexual appetite and he would now satisfy

17

The Vampire Romance Writer

his need for blood; he sank his teeth into her right jugular and drank until no life was left in her.

He then dressed left her laying there lifeless and returned to his home just before daylight he went straight and showered washing the scent of her off him.

After his shower, he went about ensuring that the sun would not reach him. After all the doors and windows were secure, he then crawled into his bed and closed the heavy curtains around the bed and drifted into a death-like sleep thinking of her.

As Dillon dressed that morning, she felt eyes upon her she went once again to her bedroom window and glanced out but saw no one. She tried to shake off the ever-increasing feeling of being watched who could be watching her anyway?

She thought that she must be getting anxious over her first vacation without her girls well she told

The Vampire Romance Writer

herself you might as well get used to it you are on your own now, the nest is empty. She turned and went back to finish dressing for work.

All during the day Dillon's mind was focused on work, it was Friday and Friday's were always busy and today was no different, car accident victims being admitted one after the next. People were in too much of a hurry to get home at rush hour causing them a hospital stay instead of a Friday night out on the town.

Dillon was always glad that by the time, she got off from work most of the traffic had died down and that night was no different. Dillon was happy to be going home thirteen hours of being on your feet could be a killer she was also glad that she had gotten a parking spot in the garage that was well lit.

During this time of year in Florida, it was still mild, but it got dark before six in the evening. As Dillon drove home, she had no feelings of being watched.

The Vampire Romance Writer

Dillon arrived home took a quick shower ate a bite and had her chamomile tea and was fast asleep.

Dillon awoke to her alarm sounding thankful that no disruptive dreams had disturbed her sleep. But as she dressed for work that morning the feeling, that someone was watching her returned.

Dillon went to her window looked out into the darkness again but saw no one she closed her eyes and thought to herself I know you're out there watching.

I can feel your eyes upon me, sending an unheard message into the darkness or so she thought. Dillon did not shake the feeling until she reached her work.

The rest of the weekend went by without any further incidents and on Sunday afternoon when she got a break at work, she had a chance to call Sarah and go over their plans for next Friday.

The Vampire Romance Writer

That is the day they would start their vacation after they finalized the last details, she hung up her cell and was back to work.

The Vampire Romance Writer

Chapter 3

During his day sleep he had dreams of her, dreams so real he felt as though he was seeing her right in front of him, she was in her room dressing in her nursing scrubs, she walked to her window looking out into the early morning darkness she saw nothing. He saw her not from her window this time but from within his mind.

He awoke that evening later than usual it was already after eight and he knew that she would already be home from work.

He was still on a high from his quest two nights before; he had stayed away from her the night following his literal devouring of that girl he did not want to take a chance of losing control of him when he got close to her.

The Vampire Romance Writer

Still unsure if he could control himself around her or not, he had to see her tonight, he dressed quickly drank down a glass of wine spiked with blood and was quickly in his jet-black sports car.

As he pulled into her apartment complex, he sensed her he could smell her sweet scent even from inside his car; he sat there for what seemed like an eternity just trying to compose himself enough to climb to her window.

He found her in her office sitting at her desk at her computer and talking on the phone, she was talking to someone he assumed that it was her daughter from the way she spoke, wishing her well at school and to make sure that she called often, then they said their goodbyes.

He continued to watch her wanting to learn all that he could about her.

The Vampire Romance Writer

How could had he had never known of
her until now, he would make it a point
to call his eternal father to try to see
why he could go all these years and
never even feel her presence.

He watched until she had finished on her
computer and readied herself for bed, he
continued to wait and watch until she fell
fast asleep before he entered her bedroom.

Dillon had the feeling again of being watched, as she
finished her conversation with her daughter and
checked her e-mail, but she did not know what to do.

Dillon had never seen anyone except for the man she
saw in the shadows at the restaurant that one day.

Dillon wondered who would be watching her anyway,
she shrugged the feeling off and went and dressed for
bed and climbed in falling asleep trying to think of
why she was having these feelings.

24

The Vampire Romance Writer

As soon as Dillon was asleep, she was thrust directly into her dream.

Dillon was in the long hall again with the pouring rain and blowing wind, the lightning streaking across the dark sky she could hear him calling Mommy! Mommy! Mommy! She ran toward his voice but no matter how fast she ran she could not reach him.

Dillon woke sat up in bed her heart racing, her breathing was fast as though she had really been running, she looked at the clock 2:30 am it would not be much longer before the clock would be sounding to wake her for work.

Dillon laid her head back on her pillows and wished for sleep to come, knowing that if it did not, she would regret it in the morning finally she drifted back off to sleep.

He watched her as she slept, and she slept soundly for a while then she started to breathe hard and he noticed her heart starting to speed up he knew she

25

The Vampire Romance Writer

was having a nightmare she was tossing and turning then suddenly she sat up in bed.

She just sat there for a moment then lay back on her pillows and eventually fell back to sleep.

He waited until he heard the rhythmic sound of her inhaling and exhaling.

When he was sure she was resting peacefully, he left her to seek out a willing or unwilling human to satisfy his desire for blood afterward he would need to find out all that could about Dillon Lane.

Monday morning came, and Dillon planned to visit her mother later that day, her mom had been disabled for a long time she lived in a retirement community in a small apartment where she had a nurse available if one was needed.

She found her mom sitting in her sunroom reading when she arrived, hi mom how is you doing? Oh, I am doing as well as can be expected just catching up on

26

some reading; they sat there and talked for a long
time Dillon asked if her mom needed anything before,
she went on her vacation.

Her mom gave her a shortlist of things that she
needed Dillon to pick up for her.

Dillon's mother was never much of one to need only
the bare essentials, as she waited for the list her
mom was making, she noted how alike she and her
mother was same strawberry blond hair, same fair
features, same freckled complexion.

Dillon even followed in her mother's footsteps in how
she never remarried after the death of her father and
Dillon never remarried after her divorce not even as
much as dating.

Dillon just found it a waste of valuable time since she
wasted the better part of her life on her one and only
marriage and she in no way going to waste any more
time on a man because at forty-two she felt that she
did not have that many more years to waste, she

27

The Vampire Romance Writer

would enjoy what years she had left on her own and alone.

Her mom finished the list and Dillon said she would run and do these errands now, and then she would return and make supper for the both of them. As she did the shopping Dillon's mind kept wandering back to her dreams, they seemed so real like she was actually there.

Dillon knew she always had been very sensitive to her emotions and most times dead on with her intuition there was a many a time she would dream about something and it would come true, but simple things like she would dream that a friend that she had not seen in ages would come to visit and sure enough within a week or two it would come true she would always chalk it up to coincidence.

Dillon was sure hoping that was not the case now the dream with the persistent man that scared her to death; she did not want to find out what he wanted.

28

The Vampire Romance Writer

As for rain, wind and lighting well that did not bother her too much she had always had those elements in all her dreams she just thought that was due to her love of the rain but the part of the dream with the child calling for her she surely thought that was her son her dead son.

Dillon finished her shopping, headed back to her moms, and prepared supper for them.

Dillon stayed and lost track of time, but she did not mind for she wanted to spend as much time as she could with her before her vacation and Dillon would be at work for the next three days then she would be gone for two weeks so it was late when she headed home.

He was a great distance away from Dillon, he could hardly stand being away from her it was as if she was a drug it only takes the one time, then you are hooked, and he was truly hooked.

The Vampire Romance Writer

His desire for her was overwhelming but he could not stand knowing why he was so drawn to her he had flown to the northeast he had asked his father to meet him maybe he could explain what was happening to him.

His father had flown from Romania just for Nicholas he would be meeting Nicholas at the hotel suite. As Nicholas arrived on his private jet his personal driver was already waiting at the airport for him Nicholas went straight to the hotel where he had a private suite, he was informed that his father was already there waiting.

Nicholas arrived and walked into the room he shook the hand of his eternal father how are you doing son? Erick asked. Things could be better Nicholas

30

The Vampire Romance Writer

replied as the butler came and poured
wine for the both of them.

They sat there for hours just catching up, so what
was so important that you have asked me to make this
long journey from Romania? Erick asked.

Well Nicholas began, you know that I have never
been one to believe that we all have a soul mate; I
had always hoped but never truly believed. All these
centuries there had never been not one-woman mortal
or immortal that have felt that I have had any
connection with, I have always longed for that special
bond that most of our kind seemed to have with their
mate.

I have always wanted it so much so that I would burn
with jealously but never, ever have I even come close
not even with Jade I loved her of course but I did
not feel that she was my soul mate.

There have been women, many women do not get me
wrong, but they were always there to fill a need
either for sustenance or pleasure, but none filled that

31

The Vampire Romance Writer

deep longing and desire for a soul mate nor have I ever sensed a woman as I do this woman that I recently encountered.

All during Nicholas's revelation Erick sat and listened patiently, then he spoke up when he had finished. His first question to his son was how did you meet this woman?

It was one morning as I was heading home after a long night I was driving through this small town in Florida.

I sensed her presence and I could smell her from a mile away, I drove in the direction of her scent and it led me to her.

As she walked past me, I just knew that there was a connection a bond it was if I had known her all my life, had loved her all my life.

The next thing I knew I was at her window just watching her. She was sitting at her computer desk, 32

The Vampire Romance Writer

she was the most beautiful woman I have ever seen, she is the complete opposite of the women that I am used to using for my needs.

I wanted this woman more than I have ever wanted anything. I felt as if I would no longer exist without her if I did not take her for mine own at that very moment.

I had the desire to take her in any way that I could I wanted her flesh and her blood, but I also knew that if I got any closer that I would lose control and leave her for dead and then I would not be able to go on.

Therefore, I kept a safe distance and continued to watch her and the more I watched the more I fell in love with her.

Well, I do not think that I should say I fell in love because I feel as though I have always loved her. However, I did not know how I could have loved her when I had never met her. My desire for her had got so intense that I had to seek out and relive my

33

The Vampire Romance Writer

frustration and desire on another mortal and in the end; I had taken that person's life. It has been a long time since I had let my rage take total control over me.

Therefore, I had to take the chance of losing her to meet with you to seek your assistance and obtain what knowledge you may have about this situation.

Being that you have lived more than twice as long as I have and hope that you may have the answers I need.

Erick remained quiet as the butler came with a new bottle of wine, they have finished the first, he started by asking exactly what is it that you want from this woman?

This should be answered first are you ready to accept this woman as your lifelong mate or do want to just use her for your pleasure, either way, you will change her life forever.

34

Nicholas sat thinking for a long time when he did speak again it was with more questions he seemed to dismiss Erick's last question because he did not think that was the solution to his problem he still could not believe that after all these years, hell after all these centuries that he was finally found his equal. How can know that she really is my soul mate?

Was his question, and how do I control myself when I am around her? How do I stop myself from totally consuming her and leaving her lifeless?

You yourself know that I have resorted to other means of sustaining myself over the years just as you have but there are the times when no other method will satisfy my thirst.

Listen! Nicholas, Erick began, you need to decide if you want to pursue having this bond with this woman, you do have a choice you can choose to let her fade back into the billions of people out in the world and remain alone, or you can take this once in lifetime

35

The Vampire Romance Writer

opportunity and go for what you have been looking for all these many centuries.

The choice is yours, as for the control issue I think that you will find that with this woman you will be able to conquer all your fears of losing control, I think that when you are close to her the love you have for her will make it impossible for you to harm her.

I also think that you will become so protective of her that you will be as if you are a shield for any harm that would come her way.

By now the sun was well on it's to being up so both men decided to retreat to the sleeping quarters. Nicholas had the suite designed so that no light could penetrate so their day sleep would not be disturbed, and he had arranged to have a fresh supply of blood stocked so that they would not have to leave the suite in their short stay there.

36

The Vampire Romance Writer

Nicholas was ready for his day rest, hoping that she would not invade his sleep because he needed a little more time to figure this situation out before heading back to Florida. Nicholas knew that if thoughts of her invaded his mind he would have to leave at once because it was taking all his strength, he had now not to go running back to her.

The Vampire Romance Writer

Chapter 4

All on arrived home she felt a sense of loneliness that she had not had in years and she did not understand why she had been divorced for about ten years and she had not longed for a companion since she had gotten over her ex-husband.

Tonight, what she felt in her heart seemed like longing for a lost love.

Her visit with her mom must have brought it on it was always hard for her after a visit with her mom because she knew deep down that her mother would never be the same.

However, something was very different this time a deeper sense of longing; she tried to push the feelings away before she became depressed.

38

The Vampire Romance Writer

Dillon decided to watch television, settled in for the night, and sat down to catch the early news before bed.

It was all the same missing children, murders, robberies, and warm weather. Soon at least she would be getting a break from the warm weather.

As she continued to watch the news, something toward the last of the newscast got her full attention.

A gruesome story about a woman that had been raped, then murdered in a hotel downtown and apparently, she had somehow been drained of all her blood.

Dillon knew that you could drain a person of all their blood but without the proper equipment that would be a difficult and messy job.

Well by the time the news went off Dillon felt sure she would have more disturbing dreams after seeing that report. Dillon was used to the blood and rape aspect after working in the medical field all these

The Vampire Romance Writer

years, but she seemed to transfer these issues into her dreams and sometimes the outcome in her dreams would be worse the than real life and that would lead to a restless night sleep.

Well, nightmares or not she headed for bed hoping at least if she did have any nightmares that she would at least have the one about the dark stranger and maybe see his face this time.

Dillon awoke this time not to her alarm clock but to her cell ringing, she glanced at the clock 4:55 am, she looked at the caller ID on her cell and it was Sarah, hi Sarah was her first words out of her mouth.

Sarah must be working on a hospice case for her to be calling at this time of the morning, and she was right.

Good morning Dillon, Sarah said, I thought you would already be up? I had five more minutes left said Dillon, so what's up? Dillon continued, oh just sitting

40

here while my patient sleeps and thought I would call you before you head to work just to make sure everything is on track for Friday.

Everything is fine on my end, how about for you? I am all ready for the cold, well I do hope we will be having a roaring fire at all times some hot men to keep us warm.

I am sure that I can manage the fire I will let you handle the men said Dillon, sometimes Dillon would wonder how Sarah and she could be friends Sarah was so much more outgoing than she was.

Dillon preferred a quiet life she liked being alone even though she was just in her early forties she had been alone for the last ten years and intended on keeping it that way but Sarah now that was a different story.

Sarah was in her early sixties and was on dates two to three times a week with men twenty to twenty-five years her junior. Dillon was sure that Sarah would try to find someone for Dillon while on their vacation.

41

The Vampire Romance Writer

But all in all, Sarah and Dillon were a lot alike they shared the same values shared the same child-raising ideas and neither of them would ever let a man rule their life we two are very strong-willed women Dillon thought.

Dillon, Dillon are you there. Sarah was saying, and Dillon came back to the present, oh yes, I just let my mind run away with me.

I best be getting off the phone and get ready for work I will talk to you later said Dillon, they said their goodbyes.

After Dillon hung up, she lay there for a few minutes longer just thinking about the man in her dreams she would be willing to give him a try, oh yeah, she thought that all the best men were the ones in your dreams. Well time to get back to reality, time for work and that was her real companion, "work".

42

The Vampire Romance Writer

Chapter 5

Nicholas was just waking up he felt very empty inside his body needed nutrition, but he also longed for her, he had to get back he could not wait any longer he must see her he would make his apologies to Erick which he knew that he would already be up.

Erick had always been able to feel the setting of the sun much earlier than Nicholas had and sure enough when Nicholas entered the living room after his shower, Erick was sitting there waiting; shall we go out this evening? Erick asked.

No, I was just coming to tell you that I have to get back to Florida and get back to her.

Erick looked at his eternal son with worry upon his face. Listen Nicholas I know that you are in a hurry to get back to her I just think that you should be as prepared as possible before doing so.

43

The Vampire Romance Writer

You have spent all of your life thinking that you would never meet your soul mate and I think that sometimes you have taken that out on other women.

I have no doubt that you will be able to control yourself around her.

However, you need to be prepared for the off chance that she does not fall under the spell that most women do when they are around you. She may not be as accepting of you as you are of her.

Nicholas had not taken that into consideration that maybe she would not be attracted to him, as he is to her.

That would be a chance he would have to take but still, he would sit and listen to Erick he did come all this way when Nicholas ask him for his assistance, his guidance.

Erick started out by telling him about how he first met Sable, Erick's wife, and Nicholas's eternal

44

The Vampire Romance Writer

mother. When I first saw her, I knew we were meant to be together and just like you, her scent would drive me insane.

It was like the most virulent aphrodisiac I have ever experienced, and I think that she felt the same thing about me but unlike Dillon, Sable was a vampire.

Sable was not so trusting of other vampires either— even if she knew that he was her soul mate she feared most vampires due to the way she was transformed.

You know the story of her transformation and what followed afterward. Nicholas knew all too well and he agreed to stay for a while longer to calm down and try to be as composed as possible because he did not want there to be any chance that he would scare her off he had to be prepared for the chance that she would not readily accept him.

Even though vampires can put people under their spell and control them to some extent he did not want to control her that way, he wanted her to want him as much as he wanted her.

45

The Vampire Romance Writer

Dillon woke early that Thursday prior to her vacation to prepare for Sarah's arrival that afternoon; Sarah was driving up from south Florida so that they could get to the airport on time the next day.

Dillon had a few errands that she had to do before Sarah got there and she had already made reservations at their favorite steak restaurant for that evening.

Dillon first would call all her daughters to check on them mostly to calm her own nerves she still had not got used to the idea that the girls would not be on this vacation.

There were no more trying to fill the vacation days with fun things for them to do, this time it would be what she wanted to do, and she still did not feel right about that. It had always been what was good for the girls, but she was trying to concentrate on her these days, and she was finding it hard to do so.

46

The Vampire Romance Writer

Chapter 6

Dillon picked up her cell first; she called McKenzie her youngest that was in college, praying that she did not have any early morning classes.

The phone ring a few times and as she was about to hang up when McKenzie answered, hi mom she said, hello sugar, Dillon said, "that's what Dillon had called her since she was a baby "I was just calling to check on you before I head out on my vacation tomorrow.

I am doing fine mom she said, don't worry about us mom just enjoy yourself and will see you on Christmas vacation.

Oh, how grown up she sounded even though she was well on her way to being an adult, but she would always be her baby.

They talked for a while longer and finally, McKenzie says she had to get to class and they ended their call with I love you's and take cares.

The Vampire Romance Writer

Then Dillon e-mailed Angelia who was in the army and stationed in an undisclosed location and told her to call when she got a chance and to be safe and she hoped that she would be able to take leave for the holidays.

Last, she called Leigh who was a driver on the NASCAR circuit, and she did reach her and again told her to be careful and to stay safe, and not to forget to be home for Christmas and she promised that she would.

After Dillon hung the phone up, she got dressed and put on a little makeup and was out the door. Dillon finished her errands and then made a quick stop to check on her mom. After she made sure that, the nurses had all on the contact numbers she was off. Back to her apartment, Sarah would be there soon.

By the time, Dillon got home and did some packing she was beat, she decided to lie on the couch and

The Vampire Romance Writer

rest her eyes and it was not long before, she drifted off to sleep.

Dillon was immediately drawn into a dream with her dark mysterious man.

Dillon still could not see his face, but she could see his eyes "pitch black", standing a short distance away from her.

Dillon could feel her blood warming up with just the touch of his eyes on her, but it was more than just his gazing upon her he seemed to be penetrating her mind with thoughts that were so exotic so erotic she could feel her body responding to his wants, his desires.

Dillon could feel his touch, a cool touch that ran down between her breasts and seemed to penetrate her chest his gaze left a cool tingling on her skin a sensation that remained even after she woke.

The Vampire Romance Writer

Dillon sat up thinking of the dream she just had and feeling as though she had just come close to having the best sex of her life, now I could take having those types of dreams, Dillon laughed at her own thoughts.

Suddenly Dillon had the feeling that she was not alone. She sat up and glanced around the room making sure her feelings were not correct and of course, there was no one there but her.

Dillon checked the time a few minutes before five.

Dillon picked up her cell to dial Sarah's number the doorbell rang she threw the blanket off her and ran to answer the door when she opened the door, she found Sarah standing there with her hands full of luggage, are you going to let me in? Or do have to stand here all night? Sarah was saying.

Dillon stepped aside and to let her in and helped her with the bags.

50

The Vampire Romance Writer

I was just going to call you, you are a little late,
well the traffic was bad, I ran into a couple of car
accidents, Sarah said, well come on in and freshen up
we have reservations for seven tonight.

Dillon helped her take her things to the second
bedroom and then Dillon went to her room to take a
bath and get dressed for dinner.

As Dillon was getting ready her thoughts, drifted
back to her dream she was thinking how it would feel
to do what she dreamed of, she was hoped it would be
as good or better in real life.

If a man could do that with just his gaze, she could
not imagine what a man like that could do with his
touch. Dillon once again found herself laughing at her
own thoughts.

Dillon did not know why she would dream such things
she was not even thinking along those exotic lines.

51

The Vampire Romance Writer

It must be my hormones in overdrive she thought, that and going without sex for years at a time will do that to you, you idiot she thought.

Maybe Sarah was right maybe she should have a little "naughty "fun while on vacation.

Dillon and Sarah made it to dinner a little late because Sarah was talking to her ex-husband on the phone, he wanted to make sure she made it here ok.

Sarah has a way with men, even after she divorces them, they still will not let her go, it is the same with her ex before this ex, sometimes one would be at her house hanging curtains and the other cleaning the pool.

Sarah even has her first husband, her children's father over for the holidays and he even stays the night sometimes, she says it is all platonic but still it did not seem normal Dillon thought. Dillon had not spoken to her ex since before the divorce.

52

The Vampire Romance Writer

Well, Dillon thought I guess some women have what it takes to keep them coming back, sometimes whether you want them to or not.

After dinner, they headed back to the apartment and made sure that everything was packed and by the door ready for the cab that would be there early then they finally settled in bed by eleven.

Dillon was praying for a good night sleep and sleep did come as she lay there thinking about her dream earlier that day.

Of all the dreams that she had recently the all-consuming dreams so real that she was sure that it would not be hard to lose yourself in them and lose sight of reality in the process.

Dillon thought to herself she should let herself have a little fun on this vacation maybe it was time to let her hair down and let go she wasn't getting any younger and if not now then when?
When would the time be right?

53

The Vampire Romance Writer

Then she thought did she really want to go through all the pain that a man can cause just to have a little pleasure.

Dillon still was not certain she always did fall fast and hard and then her heart would get broke just as fast and hard.

Well, she would have to let fate decide was her last thoughts before she drifted off to sleep.

The Vampire Romance Writer

Chapter 7

Sarah knocked on Dillon's bedroom door she was sure
that Dillon had overslept, and sure enough Dillon came
to the door all sleepy-eyed I know; I know I had a
restless night Dillon said. Well hurry and get ready I
will call the cab we don't want to be late getting to
the airport.

Dillon hurried as fast as she could, she would just
apply enough makeup to keep her from looking too
pale and try to cover up the dark circles under her
eyes.

Their flight to Denver was not due to take off until
about one o'clock but driving in the traffic to the
Orlando airport well that would take at least an hour
from her apartment than having to go through the
security checkpoints would most certainly delay them.

Dillon had just enough time to take a couple of
Tylenols for her pounding head before Sarah was
calling out to her that their cab was there Dillon

55

The Vampire Romance Writer

hurried to make sure she locked up then they were off to the airport.

Dillon was already tired, and the Tylenol had hardly touched her headache all she could think of was getting to their cabin that night and get into a cozy bed and close her eyes and mind to the world.

The flight would be a long one it would be early evening by the time they arrived then rent a car and drove to their cabin in Kremmling Colorado these were the thoughts that ran through Dillon's mind as her eyes closed and she slipped into her dream.

Dillon was standing outside a huge house, a house that she seemed to recognize but was unable to remember whose house it was.

It was almost totally dark out except for what little light that streamed from the windows.

The Vampire Romance Writer

Dillon caught a glimpse of someone in the house she slowly walked to one of the windows as she glanced inside, she saw that there was most certainly someone inside.

It was him "her" mystery man of her dreams she saw him standing there in the doorway facing the other direction he was tall had with dark hair, the clothes he wore were as if they were poured on they clung to him like a glove showing every muscle he had.

Dillon sensed that he was furious at what she was unsure of it seem that he was looking for something or someone he left the that room and continued through the house checking all the rooms his movements seemed more like he was the wind blowing through the house and his anger was building with each second that passed.

Dillon now seemed to be seeing this through invisible walls or was it through his eyes she could not tell but she felt his anger continuing to build.

The Vampire Romance Writer

As he checked each room Dillon's sense that she knew this house was getting stronger and stronger. The bed, the table, the bathroom all so familiar then she felt as though her breath had been knocked out of her IT WAS HER HOUSE!

This stranger was looking through her desk and checking her desktop looking for what?

She did not know it seemed like he could not find whatever it was that he was looking for. Then the dark stranger went to her bedroom window and let out a blood-curdling scream that sent shivers down her spine and shook her to the core.

He suddenly leaped out of her window into the night. Dillon continued to hear his scream as she woke up but realized that was not his screams but her own.

Dillon woke to people all around the plane watching her. Sarah was asking what was wrong.

The Vampire Romance Writer

There were flight attendants coming to see what the screaming was all about and all that Dillon could say was that she had a nightmare but deep down she had a feeling that there was more than some truth to her dream a lot more.

For the remainder of their flight, Dillon sat quietly Sarah did not try to speak to her for a long time when Sarah did Dillon could tell that Sarah was worried about her how are you really Dillon? Sarah asks.

Dillon thought about her dreams that she has been having lately Dillon had always thought of herself as having a touch of ESP and these dreams were along those lines, but these dreams were way too out there to be real some were downright scary, but Dillon decided to tell Sarah about them anyway.

Dillon told of the child calling out for her and of how she felt an attraction to the man in her dreams not just a sexual attraction but more of a connection, a bond!

59

The Vampire Romance Writer

Dillon went on to tell her about how she dreamed of the mysterious man searching her home and how in her dream he was calling for her to come to him and how she feared what he might do to her if she obeyed. When Dillon finished speaking Sarah looked more concerned than she did before.

Dillon; Sarah began I think that this is all because of your apprehension about finally being on your own you have spent over half you your life taking care of your ex-husband and your children.

Now that they are gone out into the world and it is just you. I think that maybe you are just a little scared and fearing the unknown.

It is a completely new life for you now and that can be a scary time in any woman's life. It's hard enough when you have a husband and

The Vampire Romance Writer

you go through the empty nest period, but you are doing this all alone the fear and loneliness is more than doubled when you face it alone.

Dillon thought about what Sarah had said and it did make sense but deep down she also knew that her instincts were usually dead on.

Dillon did not think that her dreams stemmed from the empty nest syndrome, but she did not say that to Sarah she let Sarah think that her theory could be right.

Deep down Dillon knew that whatever the meanings of her dreams were would reveal itself in time.

So maybe we can just try to forget about all of your dream drama and try to enjoy the next two weeks a couple of single available ladies all alone in all of this snow!

We need to concentrate on finding ourselves some "snowmen"? Dillon could tell that Sarah was trying to lighten the mood.

The Vampire Romance Writer

Dillon had to laugh at that and afterward her mood was lifted somewhat.

They finally settled back in their seats and discussed what they would do on their vacation.

When they landed, they collected their luggage, went to get their rental car, and started in the direction of their cabin.

They had a little way to drive until they would reach their cabin, but the drive went by fast and before long they had their high beams on and was turning off onto a snowy lane that was iced over but Dillon had the foresight to rent a S U V a four-wheel-drive JEEP. They finally made to the cabin without incident.

The Vampire Romance Writer

Chapter 8

Nicholas had arrived back in Florida just before dawn on Friday he sensed her when he got off the plane, but he knew that there would not be enough time to see her at this early morning hour. Nicholas decided to go directly to his house and straight to bed he was hoping that he would be able to rise early he wanted every waking minute that he could get to spend trying to talk to her that evening.

Nicholas did not know how much longer he could take it without her. He knew it was going to be difficult to explain to a human that vampires exist and that he was one and furthermore that he felt that she was his soul mate, he did not think that this would go over to well, but he knew he had to try.

Nicholas woke early that evening grateful for the winter months and the early sunsets.

Nicholas showered made sure to drink his fill of blood he did not want to be tempted by her scent and did

The Vampire Romance Writer

not want to be hungry for blood when he saw her, he
would satisfy that need from the packaged blood that
he gets from the blood bank.

Having the ability to influence human minds is a great
thing when you need something, and you don't want
no one to get in your way. Obtaining blood without
harming a human was easy as for his other need he
was hoping that she would be willing to help him with
that.

Nicholas was going to be there when she got from
work he did not want to approach her at the hospital
the last time he was there he noticed that she
seemed spooked going to her car he thought that it
would be better to try to talk to her on her home
turf.

Nicholas was such in a hurry to get to Dillon Nicholas
did not pay any attention to he senses for if he had
he would have noticed that he did not feel her
presence.

64

However, as Nicholas drove to her apartment, he took notice that she was not there he was hoping that she was late getting off from work.

The minutes turned into an hour Nicholas got out of his car and in an instant, he was at her door and with ease, he was in her apartment.

Nicholas could feel his anger was starting to get the best of him he quickly ran through the apartment and then stopped at her desk. He was looking for any clue as to where she might be, he turned on the computer and looked in her calendar and found what he was looking for.

She was gone, and the only information he could find on her computer was that she went to Colorado other than that he did not find any further information. Nicholas would have to call his assistant to start a search for her.

Nicholas went to her window he lifted the pane and took a deep breath trying to take in her scent he

The Vampire Romance Writer

suddenly felt overwhelmed by the fact that she was not readily within his reach.

A feeling of emptiness washed over him, he felt a sense of loss that he had not felt in a very long time he suddenly felt more alone than he had ever been.

Nicholas felt as though his insides were being shredded and he let out a cry, a cry for her.

Dillon and Sarah unlocked the cabin door they were glad to be able to get into the warmth of the cabin the caretakers had lit a fire in the fireplace for them they had called ahead and told them the approximate time that they would arrive.

Dillon did like the feel of the flames as she stood by the fireplace but after a few minutes she had to walk away, she was always a hotblooded person she could overheat in a moment's notice. Dillon had always vowed that she would move to a cooler climate when the kids were grown, and she had been thinking to

The Vampire Romance Writer

start looking for the right place, but at that moment, she thought that Colorado might just be too cold even for her hot-blooded self.

Dillon stepped away from the fire and went in search of her room she chose the one on the second floor and let Sarah take the first-floor bedroom.

Dillon climbed the stairs with her suitcase in hand and went to unpack some pajamas.

Dillon may not have enjoyed staying by the fire for extended periods of time, but Sarah was truly enjoying the warmth and after she warmed herself thoroughly, she also went to her bedroom to change.

Dillon went back downstairs after changing and found Sarah in the kitchen where there was a welcome basket on the counter, Sarah had already poured herself a glass of wine and Dillon went for a coke since she never drank alcohol.

What is the first thing that we should do Sarah ask? Well, I think that we should find a grocery store and

The Vampire Romance Writer

stock up on the supplies that we need and scout out a good bookstore.

Well, you look for the bookstore I will look for a suitable nightclub, which made Dillon roll her eyes, here we go she thought, what kind of man will she try to get for me? Dillon could only imagine.

But Dillon did say that she would try to enjoy herself on this vacation so at least she could go and check out what Kremmling Colorado had to offer in the MEN department.

Soon after both headed to bed it had been a long flight and a long drive here from the airport but before she lay down, she called each of her girls and let them know that they made it there fine and not to worry.

After she hung up, she thought that was a laugh they should be telling her not to worry.

68

The Vampire Romance Writer

Well she was here on her first vacation without them
and she was finding it hard to relax but she eventually
she dozed off after taking a couple of Tylenols pm.

Rain! Heavy rain! It was pouring out as she walked
down the long hall once again. She turned and looked
out the windows she saw that it was pouring out but
there was no sound, no sound at all it was like when
you press mute on the television.

Dillon continued walking down the hallway expecting
to see the child or her mystery man but as she
continued, she saw neither. Instead, all she saw was a
door at the end of the hall it was in the corner where
the wall was blown off previously and the door was
slowly opening.

Dillon could not understand how it could be walls don't
self-regenerate.

Dillon continued on she glanced out the window again
the rain continued to pour down.

The Vampire Romance Writer

As she got closer to the door the rain was turning into sheets of ice suddenly her ears were bombarded not with the sound of raindrops but with the sound of glass breaking it was as if a thousand windows were being thrown from the roof as the sheets of ice crashed to the ground.

Dillon saw something move in the direction of the door.

As she turned her attention, back to the door there he stood in the doorway he was the scariest thing she ever saw but also the most beautiful and even though she feared for her life she, also she felt unwavering love toward him.

Dillon dropped to her knees and started to cry so hard she thought that she would drown in her own tears. Dillon wanted to run from him and to him at the same time.

The Vampire Romance Writer

Dillon felt the most fear that she had ever felt but also the safest she could not understand how this could be.

Dillon felt as though her emotions were taking her on a rollercoaster ride to HELL.

From his appearance and how erratic her emotions were, Dillon felt as though she was in love with the DEVIL!

Dillon's eyes opened wide she looked around in the darkroom for a moment she did not know where she was then she remembered the cabin.

Dillon was shivering she saw that her blankets had dropped to the floor she picked up a throw wrapped it around her but continued to shiver as she walked to the bathroom.

Looking in the mirror "Dillon told herself" get those dreams out of your head.

The Vampire Romance Writer

She knew that the dreams initially were of her son that had passed away just after birth but now there was something more to them something she could not explain.

After having the talk with herself she eased downstairs to get something to drink Dillon poured herself a glass of water then walked over to the window she saw how beautiful it was outside with the moon shining through the bare tree limbs making shadows on the snow it sure was beautiful here she thought.

Dillon stood there a few minutes then she headed back to her room. Dillon lay down for the second time that night but this time with the feeling of fear from her dream.

Dillon lay there trying to have some understanding of her dreams and from the fear that she felt from them. Eventually, her inner voice told her that she had nothing to fear.

72

The Vampire Romance Writer

Dillon fell back to sleep with no further nightmares that night.

The Vampire Romance Writer

Chapter 9

Nicholas was on his private jet and he was due to land in Denver at any moment he knew that he would have little time to find her before first light, but he was going to try.

Nicholas had already called ahead for them to have a car waiting for him. Nicholas's assistant had done a great job of tracking Dillon down she had traveled with her friend Sarah Matthews and that was whose name the car and cabin had been rented in, so he knew exactly where to find her.

Nicholas had his things taken to the cabin that he had rented then he drove his car as quickly as he could toward her and as soon as he got within five miles of her, he not only sensed her he could smell the unmistaken scent that was Dillon.

The Vampire Romance Writer

Her scent surrounded him it was as if the cold had amplified her scent. Nicholas inhaled deeply taking in her scent when he did it made him feel as if there was an electric current flowing just below his skin making all the hair on his body stand up.

This was the first time that Nicholas had felt any spark of life since he was transformed many, many years ago.

Nicholas parked his rental car a couple of hundred feet from their cabin he sensed both women in the cabin her friend was asleep downstairs and Dillon was on the second floor he could sense that her friend was older than Dillon in years, but she had a youthful vibe about her.

Nicholas slipped through the back door of the cabin. He quietly searched the downstairs before heading up-stairs to Dillon.

With his lighting fast speed and his fine-tuned senses, he searched the whole first floor within a matter of

The Vampire Romance Writer

seconds the only thing he found was the 9mm her friend had by her bed.

Nicholas knew that that the gun would not kill him, but it could slow him down a bit.

Nicholas continued upstairs and stopped just outside her door and listen for any movement all he could hear was the rhythmic sound of her inhaling and exhaling and he had to compose himself before he entered her room.

Nicholas slowly turned the knob on her door and quietly slid into her room as he surveyed the room, he noticed that were a couple of windows in there and a small door in the ceiling that must be the entrance to a loft.

As he continued to further search the room, he saw her lying there on the bed uncovered Nicholas could feel that the room was cold he thought that she must be freezing he slipped to the bedside and knelt over

The Vampire Romance Writer

her. Nicholas could feel the heat emanating from her body.

He scanned her from head to toe her body had a bright white hue to it almost like she was glowing he had never seen anything like it before.

It was as if she had a literal fire inside her, he was so close to her that the heat from her seem to warm him, but he knew that was not possible.

Nicholas leaned forward and kissed her lightly on the lips when he did, he felt a rush of what could only be described as fire running through his body.

Nicholas felt as though his body was on fire and the longer, he kept his lips on hers the hotter he seems to get. Nicholas felt a rush of unyielding love for this woman to the like of which he never felt and never imagined that he could ever feel for any woman.

The room started to spin Nicholas could not remember the last time he felt dizzy. Nicholas felt himself fading the darkness was closing in all around him he

The Vampire Romance Writer

moved in a flash through the small door that led to the loft and was able to shut the door just before the darkness swept completely over him.

Dillon woke to a cold dark morning chilled to the bone she thought that she must be running a temperature because the only time that she felt chilled like this was when her temperature was elevated.

Dillon turned over, looked at the clock its red numbers shining brightly in the darkroom told her that was almost seven.

Dillon got up and went to the bathroom and turned the on the hot water in the tub then walked back to her bedroom to wait for the tub to fill.

Dillon walked over to the window looked out into the dark overcast morning just taking in the beautiful landscape the picturesque site that she saw reminded her why she wanted to come here for her vacation.

The Vampire Romance Writer

Dillon returned to the bathroom her bath was ready for her to submerge herself in the hot water that would surely take her chill away.

The hot water was a shocked to her, but it felt good it was what she needed to warm her.

Dillon had known that she would come down with a cold on this vacation. Dillon was never cold unless she was sick all her life, she was always extremely hot natured she never even owned a coat.

Dillon did buy a light sweater for this trip, but she only had to wear it when getting in and out of the SUV.

Living in Florida, she did not even need to wear long sleeves, so she knew she must be getting sick.

Dillon soaked in the tub until the water was starting to cool down she got out and dried off put clean pajamas on and took some Tylenol for what she knew was a fever and went back to bed she covered herself

79

The Vampire Romance Writer

from head to toe all that was peeking out was her nose.

After she finally warmed herself, she was fast asleep.

That's the way Sarah found her about three hours later, Dillon, Dillon she heard someone calling her, she propped herself up on her elbow, what time is it? She asked, almost eleven are you sick? Sarah asked.

Well, I think that I have caught a cold, well if you feel up to it get dressed and we will go check out this town and get you a cappuccino that always gives you a little pep.

Dillon dressed in a hurry, no make- up for her today just a quick brush of her teeth and put her hair into a long braid and they headed out.

When they were leaving Dillon noticed an expensive jet-black SUV parked not far from

80

The Vampire Romance Writer

the cabin along an area of the road where
there was no house's and she thought that
was strange, but she just shrugged it off
and passed by it without saying a word to
Sarah about it as they continued on their way.

The Vampire Romance Writer

Chapter 10

Their first stop was "the Country Cupboard
"she had a coffee no cappuccino there, so Dillon laced
it with milk, cinnamon, sugar and they both ordered a
full breakfast; eggs, bacon, biscuits, and gravy.

Dillon did feel a little better after she had eaten that
large breakfast and the coffee did perk her up a
little.

They sat there long after they were finished just
discussing their plans for the day.

While they sat there Dillon noticed a thirtyish
looking man that had come in, and he kept looking
over at them when he thought that they were not
looking, he was a well-dressed man, not bad looking
but not her type.

Dillon did not seem to think that he was interested
in them, in that way, no it was something else, and if

82

The Vampire Romance Writer

he continued, she would walk over there and ask him
what he wanted.

However, just before they were to leave, he got up
and left, maybe she was still spooked from all the
weird dreams that she had so she just pushed it out
of her mind.

They decided to go scout out the town. It was a
lovely town but a little too small for Dillon's likes, but
she could see herself living in a town like this if it
were just a tad bit larger, she would love to live in a
state that actually had a change of seasons.

They stopped by a small grocery store to pick up
some things that they needed then headed back to
the cabin and to rest for a while before they went out
that evening.

As they were pulling into the lane that leads to their
cabin Dillon noticed that the SUV was still there but
now there was the man from the diner looking through
the windows, he looked up as they passed.

The Vampire Romance Writer

Dillon thought that he must have broken down there and was back to get his vehicle. Maybe that is why he was looking at them earlier he must have seen them at their cabin.

They parked and went into the cabin; Dillon went straight to the fireplace to start a fire then went to help Sarah put away the groceries that they had picked up.

After they had put everything away, they went and sat by the roaring fire while they went over their plans for that night. Sarah wanted to go to this country and western bar that they saw when they were in town even though Sarah was far from a country and western woman, she wanted to check out the Kremmling men.
Dillon did not care for any bar at all, but she would go just to make Sarah happy.

84

The Vampire Romance Writer

It was settled that is what they would do they would leave about eight o'clock they would enjoy the day just sitting by the fire and reading.

They only left the living room long enough to cook them an early supper. They had decided to skip lunch since they had such a big breakfast.

Dillon was a great cook and together she and Sarah made a good hardy acorn squash soup and crusty bread, which of course that was also enjoyed by the fire.

The arrival of the night was calling for Nicholas to wake up as he aroused, he forgot for a moment where he was then it hit him, he had passed out, but how in the hell did that happen?

He had never heard of a vampire passing out, but he did, and he was still in her attic.

Nicholas noticed that it seemed to be taking a little longer than usual for him to become fully awake and

85

The Vampire Romance Writer

that too was unusual unless he had been on one of his whiskey binges.

Nicholas sat up trying to focus and it was not long before his senses were filled with the overpowering scent of Dillon. As soon as he sensed her his desire for her was taking over him, but he did not even know if he could control himself around her yet, hell he did not know if he could even stay conscious long enough to find out.

Nicholas could not take that chance and leave himself vulnerable again, so he would go and return when he had a better understanding as to what happened to him.

He could sense that both women were down on the first floor, he sat there remembering how it felt to touch her lips the sensation of warmth.

The Vampire Romance Writer

Oh! How he wanted to run and take her in his arms and kiss her neck and move to those luscious lips, damn!

He was starting to lose control again, he knew that he had to leave, and he had to leave now!

Nicholas eased the attic door open and quickly ran and into the hallway and out the window, he jumped from the second floor and landed on the ground without even making a sound.

Nicholas was in his SUV so fast that all u could see was a blur.

When he arrived at his cabin his assistant was there waiting, he had a worried look on his face. Hello Noah, Nicholas said. I was out looking for you all day when you did not arrive back here after you left the airport, I went in search of you.

I found your SUV outside Ms. Lane's cabin and I followed them into town then went back to the cabin and searched for you but saw no sign of you.

The Vampire Romance Writer

That's because I was in her attic he said, then he went on to tell him some of what happened and ask that he get him some wine and bring it to his bedroom and after he showered to get his friend Samuel on the phone, it was urgent that he speak to him.

Nicholas had to find out what was happening to him and the only man that he could think of was Samuel for he specialized in the history of vampires.

Samuel knew all that there was to know about vampires he had to find out what to do before he confronted her again.

Noah tapped on the door, then came into the room and said that he had Samuel on the line. Nicholas took the phone, hello there my longtime friend Nicholas said, hi, there yourself said Samuel in a very distinct accent that let you know that he was from Louisiana and after you heard his first words there would be no mistaking.

The Vampire Romance Writer

After Nicholas told him the story, Nicholas waited for Samuels's response, which did not come for a long time finally Samuel spoke.

It could be that someone may have placed a curse on you, what type of curse I could not say but I have never heard of a curse ever affecting a vampire before.

Nicholas was thinking over what Samuel had just said after a short pause he asked that Samuel come to Colorado to assist him in finding out what happened to him.

Samuel quickly agreed because Samuel himself had never heard of a vampire reacting the way Nick had.

I am going to ask that you have no further contact with Ms. Lane, not until I get there and can assess the situation, Nicholas reluctantly agreed.

Nick would send his private jet for him and he would be there by the next night.

89

The Vampire Romance Writer

Nicholas would soon find out that he could not wait until then because as soon as nick hung up the phone, he sensed that Dillon was with another man.

Nicholas did not know how he knew this, but he was sure that she was in danger, all vampires have heightened senses, but his senses had not been this strong before.

He bolted out the door and to his vehicle and headed toward the other end of town that is where he was sure he would find her.

The Vampire Romance Writer

Chapter 11

Dillon and Sarah arrived at the Country and Western bar just after eight.

The bar was already packed, the sign out front said that there was a dance competition that night and it seemed everyone in town had shown up by the looks of the parking lot.

All the spaces in front of and around the building were full Dillon had to park in the field at the back of the building.

Dillon hated these places, but she went along for Sarah, as they entered the bar it was hard to find a table, but they eventually found one in the far corner passed the dance floor that would give them a great view of the competition.

The Vampire Romance Writer

They sat down the waitress took their order a glass of wine for Sarah and a coke for Dillon, almost immediately a tall older gentleman asked Sarah to dance which she accepted, and it was a long time before they returned when they did the man sat down and talked to Sarah.

Dillon had a lot of the guys there ask her to dance but she was not that into dancing, but there were a couple of the electronic slot machines in the back.

Dillon excused herself, went to check them out, and when she did one of the men that were very persistent followed her there and continued to try to make conversation with her as she played, as the night went on Dillon was starting to enjoy his company.

They both enjoyed sitting there playing the slots the stranger ordered them drinks throughout the evening waiting on the chance to make his move.

The Vampire Romance Writer

He finally got his chance unnoticed by Dillon her being distracted by the machines he slipped something into her coke. Before long Dillon thought to herself you let your guard down as she started to feel lightheaded, she knew that he had put something in her drink.

Dillon looked at him unable to focus on his face she tried to call out for help, but she was unable to form any words she could only think, and her thoughts were not that clear either she repeated over and over someone please help me.

Dillon repeated this over, and over in her mind as the drug continued to slow down all her motor functions.

The man wrapped his arm around Dillon and led her out of the bar and into his truck.

Dillon tried to protest but by now, she was so weak she could barely hold her head up.

The Vampire Romance Writer

The only control that Dillon had were her thoughts and they were fuzzy, she wished that the man in her dreams were real then he could save her, these were her last thoughts before she was engulfed by the blackness that she so desperately fought to escape.

The stranger drove for about ten minutes before he turned off onto a side road, he kept glancing at her fearing she might wake up. He suspected that he had about an hour before she would wake up after she drink the coke and it had been at least twenty minutes already.

He drove until he reached a metal building that looked to be a storage facility for large trucks and equipment used to clear snow off the road.

He pulled behind the building and parked. He got out and went to the passenger's side, got her out she was able to stand with his help he knew that the drug would soon be wearing off.

94

The Vampire Romance Writer

Dillon faded in and out of consciousness she knew that she had been drugged whatever he had given her seemed to be starting to wear off, but she still was unable to regain control over her own body.

Dillon fought to stay awake she was not going to let whatever this man had in mind happen without putting up a fight.

He led her around the back of the truck she could hardly stand she was leaning on him, he had her arm wrapped around his neck she tried to break free from him, but he was too strong he let down the tailgate and laid her on the truck bed.

Dillon tried her best to keep her eyes on him as he walked back and forth around the truck.

Dillon could only wonder as to what he was doing he finally stopped at the back of the truck Dillon saw that he was starting to take off his jeans.

Dillon thought I will not let this happen to me, suddenly Dillon got a burst of energy she waited until

95

The Vampire Romance Writer

he had his jeans almost down and then she kicked him as hard as she could in the groin, and then she kicked him again in his side.

Dillon watched as he fell back onto the frozen ground then she made a break for it.

The Vampire Romance Writer

Chapter 12

Dillon went running across the snowy field behind the building toward a line of trees in the distance, but there were about four inches of snow on the ground that made running hard.

Dillon glanced over her shoulder, she saw him, and he was just a few feet behind her.

Dillon tried to run faster but he had already caught up with her. Dillon noticed that he had a large piece on a metal bar in his hand and the last thing that Dillon remembered was a sharp pain on the right side of her head before passing out.

Nicholas followed his instincts, which led him to the bar that Dillon had been but as soon as he was out of his vehicle, he knew that she was gone and that someone had taken her against her will.

Nicholas ran into the bar and immediately found her friend. Nicholas grabbed Sarah by the shoulders and started yelling where she is? Where is Dillon?

Sarah did not know who he was or what he wanted with Dillon. Sarah told him to let her go and her dance partner came and tried to get Nicholas to let her go but with one hand he flung him across the room.

Nicholas was yelling at Sarah again but by now Noah had arrived and tried to get Nicholas to calm down, Nicholas did let up a little on Sarah's shoulders Noah told Sarah that they believed that someone had taken Dillon and that the man who took her meant her harm.

Sarah told them all that she knew about the man that Dillon had been talking to over by the slot machines.

Nicholas found the waitress; ask if she knew who it was that was with Dillon.

The Vampire Romance Writer

The waitress said that she did not know his name but that he did work in the area clearing the snow off the roads, she thought he slept in a small room where they stored their machines. The waitress quickly told them where it was located.

Nicholas was out the door before anyone could say another word.

He drove at speeds reaching over a hundred miles per hour on the icy roads and when Nicholas arrived at the road that led to the storage facility, he picked up the distinct smell of blood!

Her blood!

Nicholas saw the building just ahead and within a few seconds, he was there, and out of his vehicle.

Nicholas jumped out of his vehicle and followed the scent of her blood.

The unmistakable scent of Dillon led him to a field at the back of the building. Nicholas's eyes were drawn

99

The Vampire Romance Writer

to the snow in front of him, there in the white snow was a trail of bright red blood that led across the field and into the tree line.

All that ran through his mind was that she could not be dead, not after he had finally found his soul mate.

Sarah had the gentleman take her to the address that the waitress had given them and as he drove there Sarah called the police to inform them that her friend had been taken and where to look.

When they arrived, they saw Nick's black SUV but no sign of him or Dillon or of anyone else, they both got out of the car and began looking around then they to saw the blood in the snow as Nicholas had.

Sarah started screaming and soon the police had arrived Sarah tried her best to explain what had happened, but she was hysterical her friend had to fill what he knew.

100

The Vampire Romance Writer

The police told them to return to their car; Sarah was not going to stand by while her best friend was possibly being murdered. Sarah tried to run into the woods but one of the officers stopped her.

Her friend put his arms around her to try to calm her down as he walked her back to his car and had her sit inside; Sarah just sat there in tears imagining what Dillon might be going through.

Dillon's attacker laid Dillon, all covered with blood on the frozen forest ground.

He thought to himself that he did not mind the blood it seemed to amplify his desire to want to mutilate her as he raped her.

He ripped her shirt off and then he took both hands and placed them between her breasts and grabbed her bra and ripped it off. He then reached into his pocket and pulled out his knife, cut her jeans off leaving her lying on the shredded clothes.

The Vampire Romance Writer

He then reached up to where she was bleeding and took pleasure smearing the blood over her breasts and down her abdomen and then into her hairline.

He continued to smear her blood down her inner thighs then spread her legs open and began to unzip his jeans.

The Vampire Romance Writer

Chapter 13

Nicholas was moving at the speed of light but as he followed the trail of blood, he saw each blood drop as though he was in slow motion.

Nicholas finally reached her just as the man was unzipping his jeans. Nicholas saw her laying there naked covered in her own blood, his emotions took over he felt as if his blood was boiling Nicholas grabbed the man and pulled him deeper into the woods. After Nicholas had taken him a few yards into the forest he stopped, the man was too stunned to speak.

Nicholas stared the man in the eyes as he ripped his heart right out of his chest, Nicholas then tore into this monster's throat with his long sharp fangs.

This man was too vile to even think about drinking his blood. Nicholas finally grabbed the man by the hair and ripped his head off.

The Vampire Romance Writer

By the time Nicholas arrived back to
where Dillon lay the police and medical
personnel were there, so he stayed
hidden in the shadows as they worked
on her, placed her on the gurney and
finally into the waiting ambulance.

Nicholas went back home to shower and by
the time he was dressed Noah was there
with an update on Dillon.

She was stable but in critical condition,
she had suffered a head injury but
thankfully, she had not been raped,
but she was still unconscious.

Nicholas placed his head in his hands he
blamed himself, he should have gone
straight to her when he woke, and he
should not have waited.

The Vampire Romance Writer

Nicholas told Noah to make sure that all the arrangements were made for Samuel's arrival and to meet him at the hospital in a few hours then he was out the door.

Sarah was at Dillon's bedside as soon as the doctor allowed her, and she stayed as for the entire allotted time that was allowed in intensive care.

When Sarah was not at Dillon's bedside, she stayed close by in the waiting room. Sarah decided that she would wait until morning to call Dillon's daughters, right now Dillon was stable and the doctor's said that she should recover Sarah did not want to put them through all this tonight.

Nicholas watched as Dillon's friend stood vigil over her when she left the room he came through the window, Nicholas found her lying there bruised and beaten his heart filled with love for her, he could not stand to see her hooked up to those machines she seemed so lifeless.

The Vampire Romance Writer

Nicholas wanted so much to hold her in his arms and never let her go but he was scared to touch her, scared that he would have the same reaction as before, but he had to touch her, he had to feel her life flowing through her as he eased his hand over hers it astounded him.

Her hand was not as warm as before, he still saw her white glow, but it was much fainter now.

His lips hovered over hers, but he stopped short of kissing her, instead he breathed in her scent he remained there taking in taking in all the scents that surrounded her.

She still had the scent of her spilled blood on her even though she had bathed. This made the fury rise again in him, he needed to calm down he pulled a chair as close to her bed as possible and sat there just watching her.

The Vampire Romance Writer

Nicholas did not care if someone came in, he was skilled in helping people to forget things that he did not want them to remember, as long as it was no more than one or two people at a time Nicholas had no problem of altering the memories.

It was almost dawn, Nicholas had stayed at her bedside all night but knew that he had to leave her, but he would have Noah stay and keep watch on her.

Before he left Nick once again bent over and took in her scent, this time he pressed his lips ever so slightly to hers and once again, his head was spinning, spinning so fast he thought he was going to throw up but he would not give in to the blackness, not this time.

This time he fought with all the strength that he had to stay conscious; he pulled himself quickly away from her. Nicholas walked out into the waiting room and sat in the chair next to Noah are you alright? Noah asks, you don't look so good, just a little tired that's all,

The Vampire Romance Writer

he needed to instruct Noah on what needed to be done while he was resting.

After he gave detailed instructions to Noah regarding Dillon, he made his way to his car, drove home and made it just in time, as soon as he pulled his curtains around his bed he was out.

Dusk was well on its way and Noah was waiting at the airport, Samuel would be arriving within a few minutes then straight to the cabin that was Nicholas's instructions.

Noah had worked for Nick for five years now he knew many things that would scare a normal man to death; he knew that Nicholas was a vampire.

Noah knew that there were many more vampires, but he had only been around a few but for the most part, they looked pretty normal.

The vampires never went out in the day though but otherwise, they did not bother him, as long as they

108

did not try to drink his blood and he continued to be paid well, it was just another job.

However, when he saw Samuel, he was having second thoughts, he was a tall African American man in his mid-fifties and had tattoos on his arms and neck, and he did not know why his boss would associate with him.

Each time you got a glance at him you wonder if he would bite your head off if he had the chance.

Even without knowing that he was a vampire his appearance oozed of tough, mean, no bull-man and Noah was for sure watching his back with this one.

Noah jumped out of the car and introduced himself and assisted him with his bags and held the rear door on the passenger's side open to let him in, thinking all the while, watch my back! Watch my back! Samuel spoke up and said you might want to say watch your neck!

Noah was so surprised that he did not know what to say, he had never met another vampire that could

109

The Vampire Romance Writer

read human minds; besides Nicholas, Noah would have to try to keep his mind blank around Samuel.

Noah drove Samuel to the cabin as fast as he could and tried not to think any negative thoughts, or any thoughts altogether.

When they reached there Nicholas was sitting by the fireplace drinking a glass of wine, he got up immediately to greet his longtime friend and poured him a glass of wine as Noah took his bags to his room.

Nicholas brought Samuel up to speed on the situation, and then they headed to the hospital.

110

Chapter 14

Samuel wanted to observe for himself what happened
when Nicholas touched this woman and to also see if
she had any response to his touch as he did to hers
but first, they would check on her condition.

They found her still unconscious, but Nicholas saw
improvement after Nicholas was satisfied that she was
doing better they proceeded.

If Nicholas were to pass out again then at least he
had one of the most powerful vampires ever, there to
assist him.

They started out slowly Nicholas lightly touched one
of Dillon's hands, when he touched her flesh, he went
weak in the knees, but he voiced to Samuel that he
wanted to continue.

Nicholas bent forward took in her scent,
drew himself closer to her then lightly
kissed her on her lips.

The Vampire Romance Writer

Once again, the heat from her was
overwhelming. As he continued to kiss
her, he had the sensation of what could
only be described as hot liquid wax
transferring from her to him.

Then it seemed to be circulating in his veins.

It was taking all his power not to be
dragged into the darkness that so
desperately wanted to engulf him.

Nicholas then kissed her deeply, as he
did, he was thinking that he had never
tasted anything so good in his life and
that if he did not stop and pull himself
from her, he would most certainly
devour her. That was his last thought
before the darkness finally overpowered
him.

The Vampire Romance Writer

Sarah had been at the hospital all day
she had only come back to the cabin to
shower then she was heading back to the
hospital to check on Dillon.

Sarah still had not called Dillon's family she wanted to
see if there was any improvement before doing so.
That evening after sunset, Sarah drove back to the
hospital.

When Sarah entered the ICU, she asked the nurse to
see Dillon Lane, the nurse told her that she did not
have a patient by that name in the ICU what do you
mean? I just left a couple of hours ago and she was
right here, the nurse told Sarah to hold on and she
would check to see if Dillon may have been moved to
a different room, Sarah could not understand, Dillon
was not well enough to be downgraded to a regular
floor.

 Sarah sat waiting, oh what if Dillon's condition had
worsened. What if she had to be operated on? All
these thoughts ran through her mind in the few

The Vampire Romance Writer

minutes that the nurse was gone. When the nurse returned, the nurse reassured her that Dillon was fine she had awakened and had been placed in a room on the medical floor.

Sarah felt relieved but still, she could not understand how Dillon had improved that drastically the nurse gave her the room number and she headed straight there.

When Sarah walked in Dillon was sitting up in bed looking well, so well, in fact, Sarah could hardly believe her eyes, being that she was unconscious just a few hours before and not only that she had almost died the previous night.

Dillon, how are you? I was so worried; I cannot understand how it is, that you have improved so quickly.

I really was scared that you would not make it and now look at you, you look a little drained and a few

114

The Vampire Romance Writer

bruises but that is still remarkable considering what you just went through.

I am feeling pretty good, Dillon answered, I barely feel anything, as a matter of fact, I will be leaving tomorrow morning the doctors just want to run a few more tests, as usual, but really, I feel fine.

Dillon asks if Sarah had contacted her daughters and Sarah informed her that she was going to do that this evening after she checked on her.

Dillon told her not too that she would call them herself as soon as she was discharged, she did not want to have them worry when there was no need.

Sarah did not want to bring up what happened, afraid that Dillon might get upset but she wondered if she remembered anything about that night; the police would be asking her questions.

Sarah was not going to tell Dillon how they found the man that attacked her; apparently, he was interrupted by a wild animal and torn to pieces.

115

The Vampire Romance Writer

At least that is what the police think, none of that matters right now her main concern was Dillon's health, which she seemed to be getting better with each passing moment.

Nicholas woke three hours later, he found himself back at home lying in bed with Samuel standing over him chanting words he could not understand.

Nicholas sat up and asks how long he out was, Samuel told him, so what do you think?

What is going on?

Samuel has studied vampires for centuries trying to see what would harm them; what would make them stronger, weaker.

He had seen how Nicholas had reacted with Dillon's touch; it seems as though you are experiencing something like an electric jolt from this woman's touch.

116

The Vampire Romance Writer

Almost like having a defibrillator used on you but of course, we know that the real defibrillators do not work on vampires. Essentially, though I think that what her touch does to vampires is give them an unusual electrical jolt, kind of like a jump-start to your life force that has been absent for many years.

It is not only the electrical jolt; she somehow seems to increase your body temperature in the process.

My initial conclusion is that this woman holds a power that allows her to bring life back into vampires once again.

Samuel had never heard of this but with what he witnessed tonight well what else could it be.

Samuel finished giving Nicholas his analysis of what he had seen so far.

Samuel also took notice that she did seem to be Nicholas soul mate, that in itself is a powerful bond but when you are soul mates with a woman that can

The Vampire Romance Writer

bring life back into a vampire, is not only a powerful combination but also extremely dangerous.

However, of course, he would need more time to test his theories. After listening to all that Samuel had to say Nicholas was stunned, to say the least, and then the reality of the situation hit him. Nicholas knew if any other vampires found this out, she could be in danger.

Nicholas sat up on the side of the bed, still feeling a little faint he placed his hands to his head trying to stop it from spinning.

What kind of reaction did Dillon have when we touched?

As far as I could tell she had no reaction at all, her heart rate stayed the same there were no fluctuations at all in any of her vital signs.

The Vampire Romance Writer

Nicholas finally felt that he could stand without passing out, he got up and walked to his window and opened the heavy sun blocking blinds.

Nicholas stared out into the cold night, thinking that he is as dead as the vegetation that lies underneath all that snow and ice. Except unlike him, the vegetation will regenerate with the warmth of the sun come spring but there was never any spring for him he never had the option to regenerate, to live, never even thought it was possible.

Nicholas always wished that he had not been turned into a vampire, wished that he had lived as a normal human being, but fate took that decision out of his hands and he had to live with it forever.

This new revelation that he could possibly be human again was definitely a turning point in a direction that he wanted to take.

The Vampire Romance Writer

Chapter 15

Dillon was released from the hospital the next
morning. She was as surprised as Sarah and the
doctors of her rapid recovery, but she made no
mention of this to either of them.

Sarah wanted to go back to Florida right away, but
Dillon flat out refused she was not going anywhere.

Dillon wanted answers and she knew that she had to
stay here if she wanted those answers, answers to her
many questions.

The police had questioned Dillon that morning before
she left the hospital, they ask her question after
question about what had happened.

Dillon told them all that she could remember was that
she had met the man at the bar and those they had

The Vampire Romance Writer

played the slot machines together and after she had a couple of drinks, she felt that she was possibly drugged.

She remembered him taking her to his truck, she remembered trying to escape, and after that, she did not remember anything more until she woke up in the hospital.

The detectives told her that they would be in touch if they had any more questions.

Dillon was letting the police and Sarah think that she did not remember anything more about that night, but she remembered everything.

Dillon remembered laying there naked on the frozen ground not able to move and having her own blood smeared all down her naked body.

She remembered almost being raped and most of all she remembered the tall dark handsome stranger from her dreams saving her.

The Vampire Romance Writer

Dillon remembered the torture on his face when he saw her lying there all bloody and naked covered in her own blood about to be raped and most certainly killed.

Dillon remembered the anger that took over him, as he grabbed the man and practically flew into the woods and somehow deep down, she knew that he killed her would-be rapist; her would-be killer.

Dillon also remembered him in her hospital room he was kissing her, and she remembered feeling as though ice water was running through her veins with the touch of his lips, but she also felt confused because she felt love for him.

A love that seemed she had always had and would have forever, not only love through a connection a deep connection.

The Vampire Romance Writer

Dillon would stay she needed answers, and this was the place to find them she was sure but how to find them was the question.

The drive to the cabin was a quiet drive with Sarah afraid to say anything afraid that she might upset Dillon and Dillon's mind was still trying to sort it all out; her dreams had been trying to warn her that she knew for sure. Dillon needed to try to remember all that she could about her dreams and try to see what else they may have been trying to tell her.

As soon as they arrived at the cabin Dillon excused her and went straight to her room, Sarah yelled out to her saying that she would bring her up a cup of tea.

Dillon headed straight to her "I Pad" looked up all that she could about the incident, she was right her attacker had been killed; he had apparently been mauled to death by a wild animal shortly after kidnapping her.

The Vampire Romance Writer

Dillon knew better than that she knew that her mystery man had something to do with his death as these thoughts ran through her mind, she suddenly felt the need to take a hot bath.

Dillon had seen many rape victims in her life and now she understood why they wanted to go straight and shower; even though Dillon had not been raped, she could still feel his grimy hands on her.

Dillon could still feel him smearing her own blood all over her, like the sting of a wasp the stinging sensation lingers long after the wasp is gone.

Dillon decided that she would take one of the muscle relaxers that the doctor prescribed, that combined with the hot water she hoped that would help her achy muscles, even though she was recovering pretty quick she was still quite sore.

As Dillon stepped in the hot soapy water, it covered her up to her chin she immediately began to relax but

The Vampire Romance Writer

she could not help but let her mind wander back to that night, to the man that saved her. Why had he gone so far as to kill her attacker?

Dillon knew that the news report was wrong that was no animal, it was the dark mystery man of her dreams.

Dillon was dozing in the tub when Sarah called up to see if she was about ready for her tea, she called back and told her to give her a few more minutes.

Dillon got out and dried off then turned and looked at her reflection in the mirror and thought that she was bruised literally from head to toe; the blow to her head gave her a nice egg on her right side of her head. The accumulated blood under her egg-shaped bump was dispersing and giving her a nice black eye but overall, she did not feel as bad as she thought she should.

Sarah arrived with the tea just as Dillon finished putting on her pajamas, how are you feeling?

125

The Vampire Romance Writer

Better, the hot bath helped wash away more than just dirt, are you sure, you don't want to go home? Sarah asked,

No, no I think I need to be here at least for a little while longer, she asked Sarah to sit and have tea with her.

Dillon decided that she would confide in Sarah about her dreams and what happen when she was kidnapped.

When Dillon finished, she could not tell if Sarah believed her or if she thought that all of this was from the concussion, she had but Sarah did agree to stay and finish the vacation with
Dillon.

Dillon and Sarah stayed in the cabin all that day Dillon napping throughout the day and Sarah checking in on her, toward that evening Dillon called her children and gave that an abbreviated version of what had happened to her.

The Vampire Romance Writer

Dillon reassured them that she was fine and that she would be home in a couple of weeks.

As night fell, Dillon went downstairs and built a fire while Sarah made dinner so how are we going to find out anything about your mystery man? Sarah asked, well I think that somehow, he comes to me in my dreams.

Sarah gave her a worried look, oh don't get worried I am not crazy you are supposed to be keeping an open mind. Sarah motioned her to the table where she was serving up steaming bowl of potato soup and crusty bread. They sat down to their dinner, Dillon commenting on how delicious the soup was Dillon was hoping to ease Sarah's mind by making small talk.

Dillon still could see that her friend was worried, and she could tell that she still felt guilty that she was not able to protect her the night that she was kidnapped.

The Vampire Romance Writer

They finished the rest of their dinner pretty much in silence, Sarah insisted that Dillon relax as she cleaned up, Dillon did as she was told.

Dillon went and sat in front of the fireplace and grabbed her "I Pad "she would continue her search on any information about her attacker.

Dillon hoping there would be something that would lead her to her knight in shining armor, but there was nothing that was out of the ordinary other than the fact that the police have it all wrong.

Finding nothing else she decided to head to bed but before she did, she checked all the doors and windows before telling Sarah goodnight when she reached the top landing, she also checked the window there and each one that she passed then finally her own.

Dillon stopped in front of the window glanced out over the property, the snow was already a few inches deep and the forecast called for more.

128

The Vampire Romance Writer

Any other time Dillon would have enjoyed the snow she had always enjoyed the cold weather but tonight when she looked out into the cold snowy night, she had a wave of depression sweep over her. Dillon quickly closed the curtains, walked into the bathroom and took a couple of muscle relaxer's and went to bed. Dillon decided to leave a light on in the bathroom, letting the light spill softly into the bedroom after what seemed like hours, she fell asleep.

The Vampire Romance Writer

Chapter 16

Nicholas rose with the setting sun and called down for Noah. Contact my father and ask him to come, also have my home in Denver ready for me by morning, yes sir was all that Noah had said before he left the room.

Nicholas took a shower and went downstairs to meet with Samuel of which he knew would already be wide-awake. Nicholas found him sitting by the fireplace, good evening Samuel evening Nicholas.

I was thinking that you should go and stay at my house in Denver it is a much larger place than this and with my father on his way to Colorado, this place is too small.

I think that we will be staying in Colorado for a while longer, Samuel agreed, so I assume that you will be staying here tonight.

130

The Vampire Romance Writer

Nicholas hesitated, before answering; yes, Nicholas replied, I need to be as close to Dillon as possible. It will take me some time to set up the protection that I know she will need, and I need you to try to find out all you can about our unique situation without raising any red flags.

I assume you will be seeing Dillon tonight Samuel said, yes that is the plan, well please take caution not to touch her.

Nicholas was thinking how he was going to accomplish that because that is all that he wanted to do when he was around her, but he did say that he would try then he was out the door.

Nicholas watched as she checked all the locks and as she stood at her window just looking out into the darkness. As she closed the closed curtains, he could feel that she was scared but she tried to hide that from her friend and that made him wonder why she had not gone back to Florida.

The Vampire Romance Writer

When Dillon was asleep Nicholas went to her bedside careful not to touch her, laid down beside her on the bed willing her not to awake but not knowing that his powers of persuasion had no effect on her.

As he lay there, he could feel the heat emanating from her body, which sent a warm feeling through him the feeling he had not felt since being human.

Nicholas lay there letting his mind wonder about this woman that he had no doubt was his mate, ever since Nicholas had found Dillon he had been experiencing more and more of his previous human functions he thought to himself that he would graciously accept the gift of being human again if she wanted to give it to him.

Laying there beside Dillon seemed so right it seemed as though this is where he should have been all along. That is where he stayed right beside her all night until just before dawn, he left her with the silent promise to return to her that night.

The Vampire Romance Writer

Dillon, he had slept well except for a few times she thought that she might have had a nightmare but otherwise she slept soundly. Dillon was grateful to finally get some sleep.

It took Nicholas longer to get to his house in Denver, so he had to leave sooner than he wanted but he needed to be there when his father arrived, and he would return that night to be by her side again, he knew he would be by her side forevermore.

With his father, coming Nicholas knew that his mother Sable would be along soon.

Nicholas arrived at his house, which was a large mansion situated on the outskirts of Denver. The house looked as though a king might live there, that's the way he liked it, the old-world style he loved the big columns and the high ceilings that this place had but he did not like being here all alone, it was much too big for one.

133

The Vampire Romance Writer

Nicholas pulled up he could the presence of his father, he was inside waiting, hello son Erick greeted him, hello father.

Nicholas filled his father in on the situation and confided in him that he knew for sure that Dillon was his soul mate but what good was having someone as your soul mate if you could never feel her touch, never be able to hold her in your arms.

Erick placed his hand on his son's shoulder we will figure this out but until then I think it wise that you follow Samuels advice and not to have any physical contact with her.

Nicholas promised his father and sat down to have a glass of wine just before they parted ways to their bedrooms.

Dillon slept well she told Sarah, but it was a different sleep, it was interrupted but not in the usual manner as before.

134

Dillon had slept well but her dreams returned. The rain; the long hall, and her dark mystery man.

He was waiting for her at the end of the hall with its corner blown off, but she had no fear of him, as she walked closer to him, she glanced out the windows.

The rain was pouring out and just as before, the further she went down the hall the rain turned in to ice, she kept her eyes on the ice as she was walking down the hall.

When she turned around, he was standing right in front of her, just standing.

Dillon said not a word not because she was scared, she was mesmerized, his eyes were truly pitch black and he was the most handsome man she ever saw.

There they stood for what seemed like hours then he spoke. I have been waiting centuries for you and then suddenly he disappeared.

The Vampire Romance Writer

Well, Sarah said, at least the dream seems to be improving them both laughed at that.

Nicholas came back each night lying beside her and each night fighting his desire to touch her, fighting the urge not to take her in his arms and make love to her, he would lay so close that he could feel the heat from her body, could feel the life in her wanting to jump into him. He worried that somehow the life that wanted in him would kill him in the end.

Each night Dillon would take her medicine and each night she would have the same dream they seemed so real to her she knew that he was real, and he had come to her before in her dreams than in real life.

Suddenly it hit her tonight she would not take the muscle relaxer and see if that made any difference in her dream.

Dillon lay down, but it took a little longer than before to fall asleep with nothing to help her ease off to

136

The Vampire Romance Writer

sleep but around midnight she finally drifted off to sleep.

Nicholas noticed a change in Dillon she seemed restless that evening but as soon as she fell asleep, he was at her bedside in an instant and took his place beside her ever so close he inched. Nicholas watched as her chest rose and fell softly. He had a lot of time to think about how he was to approach her. He could not just knock on her door and say hi I am Nicholas Logan and I am a vampire and I am in love with you and I have looked for you for most of my life.

Well, he would have to think of something soon she needed to know about the powers that she had.

The power to possibly bring life to a vampire was not something that stayed a secret for long.

Tonight, Nicholas would have to meet with his father he would not be able to stay long. As he was getting up to leave he brought his lips within millimeters of her longing to kiss her, he whispered in her ear, I

The Vampire Romance Writer

have to leave you for tonight, my love, but I will
return until then sleep soundly, his last words were
more of a command as he was willing her to do so.

As Nicholas rose up and turned toward the window,
he heard her say don't go he turned on the spot
looked her in the eyes she was awake wide-awake
reaching for him.

The Vampire Romance Writer

Chapter 17

Dillon's sixth sense was telling her that when she took the muscle relaxer it made, he falls into a deeper sleep and during this period of deeper sleep he would come to without her knowing. Now that the muscle relaxer was not, in her system, she had more control of her mind and tonight she was going to test her theory.

Dillon was in one of her dreams he was still standing in the hall telling her how he had been waiting for her for centuries and then he turned to go, she reached for him she told him not to go.

Dillon woke up and he was there in her room leaving! She called for him to wait don't go, he turned quickly toward her. All of a sudden Sarah was at her bedroom door with her 9mm, the gun fired as Nicholas turned toward Sarah, he was in front of her within a second ready to attach Dillon was screaming no.

The Vampire Romance Writer

Dillon grabbed his arm and as she did within a second, she watched as his eyes rolled back into his head and he passed out, landing at her feet on the floor.

Sarah was screaming, Dillon told her to calm down, calm down. What do you mean calm down? I just killed a man they both bent to check his wound you just missed his heart, Dillon said. There is very little blood, grab a towel and place it over his wound, Dillon told Sarah.

Sarah ran for the towel and placed it over the bullet hole then she felt for a pulse, she felt none. Sarah started screaming he is already cold, oh my god, oh my god, we have to call for an ambulance.

Sarah reached for the phone, but Dillon got to her before she could dial, he is not dead at least not in the manner in which you think.

The Vampire Romance Writer

What do you mean in the manner, I think? As far as I know, there is only one kind of dead and that's "Dead", not breathing, no pulse and a big bullet wound in his chest that spells dead to me. Come and I will show you.

Dillon had known as soon as she saw him what he was, look she said to Sarah he is healing as we speak, he is alive just, unconscious and he is unconscious not from your bullet but somehow from my touch. I remember he did the same thing at the hospital.

He is a vampire said Dillon, Sarah looked at Dillon, I am calling the ambulance for you and him you are totally nuts and I am sitting here listening to you talk out of your mind while he lays there dying. Let me show you something Sarah, I don't know nothing about vampires, damn I did not even think that they were real but what else could he be.

He has been coming to me each night since my attack and until tonight I thought he was only coming to me in my dreams but tonight I realize he has been

141

The Vampire Romance Writer

here in real life and in my dreams, he is a vampire and so far, my dreams have been right on target.

Nevertheless, if he is a vampire how is it that he is laying here unconscious on your bedroom floor?

Well I think that their blood is cold, and it runs slowly through their veins and somehow when I touch him, he is warmed by my touch and his blood warms up and in turn, it runs faster, and he faints from the sudden rush of blood to his brain.

You check his pulse and I will hold his hand and let's see what happens, he does not have a pulse Sarah reminded Dillon.

Just do it, Sarah, Sarah did as she was told when she touched him, he was cold. Sarah searched and searched for a pulse, finally she felt a very faint pulse.

Sarah watched as Dillon touched him and immediately, she felt his pulse speed up and it was much stronger.

142

The Vampire Romance Writer

Dillon got up and ran to her bags in her closet; Sarah screamed where are you going? Don't leave me alone with a bloodthirsty vampire who is more than likely thirsty for my blood since I just shot him.

Dillon called back you cannot kill him with a bullet.

Dillon always kept a supply of smelling salts with her; you could not imagine how many people fainted these days.

Dillon ran back to the bedroom what are you doing? Sarah asked I am going to wake him, oh my god you are definitely going to get us killed!

Dillon turned to her, I do not think he wants to hurt us, I have been dreaming of this man for months and he is the one that saved me from that kidnapper.

I also think that he is in love with me and I think that he has been coming to keep me safe during the night.

The Vampire Romance Writer

So please just stand back while I try this, but before I do, Dillon had the urged to kiss him, she leaned forward and pressed her lips to his, cold but soft she thought, then she heard him take a breath, then another, then he seemed to be having a seizure.

Dillon stopped kissing him, he continued to twitch a little but as soon it started to calm down.

What the hell are you doing? Sarah yelled, just sampling. Dillon cracked the small vial and placed it under his nose, nothing happened.

Dillon kept it there it took a little longer than it does for a human to wake up but after a few minutes, he started to stir.

He looked up at her, sat straight up, and grabbed his chest. Who shot me? Were his first words out of his mouth, you could see the anger building in his eyes.

Sarah did, Dillon answered nodding in Sarah's direction the fear on Sarah's face was so prevalent she

144

The Vampire Romance Writer

had the gun pointed this time dead on at his heart, but she did it only to protect me. Nicholas was up in an instant and started toward Sarah, but Dillon stepped in front of him like I said she thought I was in danger.

Dillon looked deep into his eyes and she could see the love that he had for her, he then placed his hands to his forehead I feel dizzy.

Dillon motioned him to a chair what time is it? Almost five, I must go, but you cannot go in this condition you are still bleeding. I will be fine, No! Dillon said you will stay she commanded him.

Never had a woman spoke to Nicholas like that and lived but this woman she had more than one power over him.

If it was not so close to dawn he would stay, damn how he wanted to stay.

Nicholas made a move to leave and Dillon was expecting it, she had already had this planned out.

145

The Vampire Romance Writer

Dillon reached out and grabbed his hand, and just like that, he was out.

What are you doing? Wake him back up, wake him Dillon and let him go. No Dillon screamed at Sarah, not until I have some time to think, you cannot keep him here as a pet Dillon.

I know that Sarah just help me put him on the bed until I can make better arrangements.

After they got him on her bed Dillon ran to the hall, she knew that there was a small storage room there, which did not have any windows.

Dillon remembered from all the books that she had read and the movies she watched, that vampires could not be in sunlight. Dillon did not know if that was true or not, but she was not taking any chances.

Dillon laid down a couple of quilts on the floor and then threw in some pillows and she and Sarah placed

The Vampire Romance Writer

him on the quilts, she covered him with another quilt and pulled the door shut.

Sarah grabbed Dillon by the shoulders, listen we cannot have him here, I am sure that one of his kind will miss him and come looking for him.

Dillon slowly removed Sarah's hands from her shoulders, it will be this evening before he wakes and if he is truly a vampire and if the information about vampires rising with the sunset is correct then I have all day until he or any of his kind awaken.

He can leave when he wakes but until then I want to do some research.

Dillon left Sarah standing in the hall and went to make her a cup of cappuccino. Sarah went following right behind her, I know you too well Dillon I can tell that you have feelings for that man or whatever he is.

Dillon did not say a word she pretended that she did not even hear Sarah.

The Vampire Romance Writer

Sarah faced Dillon do not tell me that you love that, that vampire, you who swore that she would never love again.

Dillon turned away, I am not saying that I love him, but I do feel a strong connection, a very special connection at that, so if you will excuse me, please.

Dillon passed by Sarah and went to get her "I Pad".

Dillon researched all morning on anything that she could find on vampires and on returning vampires human again, not knowing if any of it were true.

Dillon continued her research until Sarah called her for lunch. As Dillon sat down, Sarah asked should we not go and check on him again. I do not think I want to continue to keep going in there I do not want to risk any sunlight reaching him.

Do you think that the sunlight thing is real or what? Well, I think we should take all the precautions that

The Vampire Romance Writer

are necessary just in case it is but so far, each time
I had checked he was still out cold.

I will go in just before it gets dark, I want to try
something. What exactly what are you going to try?
Well, I think that somehow when I touch him it
brings life into his lifeless body and that is why he
reacts the way he does.

I do not know for sure, but I think that their
metabolic system operates at a very minimal level and
when the sun raises its drops their metabolic rate
even further.

If I am right, I think that when I touch him during
this time, he will be able to handle it better and
might not pass out, don't you think that you may
harm him? Well, he is a vampire I think he can
handle a little shock to his system.

I have a feeling that I am supposed to somehow use
this power to bring some type of life back to the
vampires.

The Vampire Romance Writer

Chapter 18

Around four o'clock Dillon had Sarah help her block out all the light from the windows.

Dillon slowly entered the storage room; she had a small lamp with her that gave off just enough light to light her way to him.

Dillon sat the lamp on the floor; he looked as if he had not moved a muscle.

Dillon knew that she had to do this just right, somehow, she knew deep down that this was what she was supposed to do, she could not explain how she knew but she just knew. First Dillon placed her hand on his wrist and checked his pulse she noted that it was speeding up with just her of her hand.

The Vampire Romance Writer

Next Dillon removed his shirt and saw that his wound had healed completely, this is crazy, crazy, crazy she thought to herself what am I doing?

She sat there beside the man that had been haunting her dreams for a few minutes trying to decide if she really wanted to go through with what she had been planning all day.

Suddenly she jerked her own shirt off and straddled his waist then she slowly laid on his chest to chest with nothing between them.

Dillon could feel the heat from her body flowing into him she could feel a slight vibration as she let her heat flow into him. After a few minutes, she reached for her smelling salts and placed it under his nose and after a minute or two, he started slowing waking up.

Dillon noticed his eyes start to flutter then suddenly his eyes opened wide then he grabbed both of her wrists with such force she thought he would snap them both.

He looked dazed; when he was able to focus, he realized that it was Dillon. He just stared into her eyes her not saying a word, he loosened his grip on her, but he did not let go completely he slowly raised himself to a sitting position.

Nicholas was just amazed that this beautiful woman was just sitting there not saying a word, and her touch was not having any effect on him but instead of asking her how that was possible he pulled her toward him and began kissing her so forcefully she thought that he would devour her. Dillon felt a hot sensation rush over her.

The hot sensation was followed quickly by a cold sensation both of which increased her desire for more.

Nicholas was having the same feeling but for him but in reverse, he felt the cold wash over him then he felt the warmest sensation run through his entire body.

152

The Vampire Romance Writer

With what seemed like the speed of light he had stripped her naked within a few seconds and he took less time than that for him to rid himself of all his clothes.

As his naked body touched hers, it seemed that every cell in his body turned to hot metal, his blood lava.

It was as if their bodies were molding into one, he had never experienced pleasure like this with another woman or vampire before.

He pulled her to her knees as she continued to straddle him enjoying his passionate kisses. He slowly entwined his fingers in her long hair, pulled her head back exposing her beautiful neck. Nicholas kissed her neck so softly, just below her ear lobe then down under her chin.

Nicholas cupped her breasts one, in each hand then lowering his mouth to one suckled as if she could give him the nectar of life.

The Vampire Romance Writer

Dillon had never felt such desire for a man, never felt such passion as she was feeling at that moment.

Dillon ran her hands through his thick black hair as he nibbled at her nipples, she felt the need to have him inside her. A desire so strong her body seemed to be crying out for him.

Dillon needed him to fill her, she raised herself up, and then slowly she lowered herself onto him feeling his coldness filling her.

Dillon moved slowly, she felt him wanting her to move more quickly but she resisted and rode him slowly, feeling a rush of coldness followed by pure heat each time she drove herself down onto him.

It had been a long time for her and she was savoring every minute of it, but she was driving him crazy, he wanted to take her fast and hard, wanted to lift her up and pump her hard on him but he let her stay in control, he let her take him as she pleased. The way

154

The Vampire Romance Writer

she moved was like having a drawn-out orgasm, the sensation she was giving him was so pleasurable, no words came to mind to describe it.

He could feel the orgasm building not only in him but her as well, she suddenly clamped her mouth over his and kissed him as if she would devour him and he returned her kisses with equal force then he felt her wave of release and as she climaxed he heard her let out a little sigh of pleasure.

He felt himself coming to a climax it was like an explosion inside of him, an explosion of life.

As their kisses slowed down, she released the grip that she had on his lips as he laid back onto the bed with her still on top of him Dillon laid her head on his chest and they just laid there not saying a word to one another. Dillon had never been as satisfied as he had just made her, there seemed to be a deep, deep connection that she could not explain.

How? How? Did you awaken me? Moreover, how is this happening?

155

I should not awaken for at least an hour.

This string of questions was what broke the silence.

Dillon ignored his questions and raised her head up off his chest to look him in the face.

Well, do you mind if we can start with introductions first, my name is Dillon, Dillon Lane but I have the feeling that you already know that and what I may ask is yours? Can please tell me exactly what you are?

Nicholas looked at her, I am Nicholas Logan, I am a vampire and I have waiting centuries for you.

Nice to meet you was Dillon's only reply; she raised herself up off him and rolled over to lie beside him.

Nicholas expected her to be shocked; surprised, something, but she showed nothing, he found himself the one surprised.

156

The Vampire Romance Writer

Well, Dillon started out, I do not know how exactly but somehow when I touch you, my touch seems to speed up your heart rate and it also seems to warm your body and you awaken.

When this is done during your normal waking hours you are overstimulated and the blood flow rushes too fast to your brain, which that causes you to lose consciousness.

However, if this is done in your resting state when your blood flow is practically stopped, and you have a stimulant to wake you those two in combination allows you to withstand my touch and you are awakened.

He listened to her theory and it all made sense, but he knew that there was more to it, more that lay deeply hidden and that's what he needed to find out.

Nicholas needed to know what force in her made this possible; he knew that there was much, much more to be learned from this situation.

Nicholas dressed and led her to her bedroom; Dillon excused herself and went to the bathroom to freshen up.

When Dillon returned, they walked downstairs where Sarah was waiting with a scared look on her face.

Nicholas knew that Sarah had her loaded 9 mm in her pocket; there is nothing to fear he told her.

I do not hold what you did against you, I know that you were trying to protect Dillon and for that, I am appreciative.

Sarah looked at him in disbelief but nodded her head toward him.

Nicholas turned to Dillon I will go for now, but we will meet again soon and then we will need to make some decisions on what we are to do next.

Dillon also nodded her head in agreement, until then she said, until then he responded.

158

The Vampire Romance Writer

They did not dare touch for fear that he would be back on the floor.

Dillon walked him to the door then he was gone into the dark cold evening.

The Vampire Romance Writer

Chapter 19

You would have thought the first question from Sarah would have been, did your theory work?

But no, it was well did he bite you? Dillon turned and looked at her and said with a laugh, no he did not, he did something much better than that, as she turned and went to the kitchen.

Well spill it then, there is nothing to tell I woke him, and we have a few minutes of, Dillon stopped, a few minutes of pleasure and discussed the reaction that I have on him.

Sarah was not standing for such simple answers, I want details, is he really a vampire?

Would the sun kill him if it touched him? Is he really dead?
Yes, yes and yes, was Dillon's answer.

160

The Vampire Romance Writer

Oh my god! Were the only words that Sarah uttered as she sat down next to Dillon.

Listen, Dillon, I am scared; of this whole situation, we do not know a thing about this situation.

If the situation you are referring to is him being a vampire,

I know that we don't, and I am sure not many people in the world does, but I can tell you this much, we are meant to be together he and I and I am going to try my best to find out all that I can about him.

I am going to do some research into why I have the effect that I do on him.

I would really appreciate your help on this.

Sarah just sat there silent for a few minutes and finally spoke up; yes, of course, I will be here to help you what are friends for? Nevertheless, can we please be careful we do not even know who he really is.

The Vampire Romance Writer

Dillon got up and walked over to Sarah and gave her a big hug, thanks to Sarah this really means a lot.

As Nicholas entered his house his father and Samuel were there waiting, they both asked in unison where have you been?

We were worried! Noah said that you were supposed to be back here before dawn.

I will speak to both of you in a little while, let me freshen up then we need to discuss some things, meet me in my private study in an hour.

Bring some wine and my special mixture to my room, he told Noah and we are not to be disturbed when we start. Noah nodded and left the room to go do as he was told.

Nicholas went to his bathroom and took a long hot shower his thoughts on Dillon.

The Vampire Romance Writer

Nicholas would need to protect this gift of hers, it also would need to be studied and he must not let this get out for he knew that Dillon would be in danger if it did.

Hell, she may already be in danger, he did not know if anyone knew about this kind power, he himself had never heard of it and Samuel also had never heard of it, but just because they had not he could not take the chance and naively think that no one else had either.

Nicholas finished his shower, dressed in dark blue jeans, a white buttoned-down shirt and boots then headed to the sitting area in his room where he found the wine and his special drink that he produced himself, a mixture of the finest wine and blood mixed. For Nicholas, this minimized his thirst for blood.

Nicholas took his special blend to the study with him, his father and friend were both there waiting by the fire.

The first thing that I want to make clear is that

The Vampire Romance Writer

Dillon Lane will be my wife! And from now

on, she is part of this family human or not. Samuel
and Erick nodded in agreement.

Nicholas continued; I have found out that she can
somehow awaken a vampire during our sleep of
renewal. Both elder vampires had a look of disbelief;
they both started to say something, but Nicholas held
up his hand and ask them to please wait.

Nicholas continued, it seems that she may also be
able to bring some aspect of life back into vampires,
to what extent is yet to be seen but from my own
experience it seemed like I had life flowing through
my veins once again.

I felt a little of my human self, returning but not
just human, but a superhuman, super vampire all
rolled into one.

Samuel and Erick sat there in silence for a while they
seemed as if they were searching for words, they did
164

The Vampire Romance Writer

not want to pry too much but there were questions that needed to be asked.

His father started with the first question.

How did she awaken you son? Nicholas did know where to start, but he proceeded cautiously.

With her touch, she was able to warm my blood, and this caused my blood to flow faster.

When that happens, I will lose consciousness if this is done in my normal awaken hours but if this is done during the times that are body is in its renewal state, she was able to wake me without causing me harm.

I seem to have no ill effects from her touch during this time. Dillon had used the Spirit of Hartshorn to bring me into consciousness after she had warmed me with her touch.

As for how the process works and what underlying force, is giving her the power to warm my body and awake me I do not know.

165

The Vampire Romance Writer

I do sense a power in her, but no power that I have ever felt before, where is this power from? I do not know this either, is what we need to find out.

We also need to find out if, any harm is being done to me in the process or if there are any lasting side effects for either of us.

Samuel I will need you to set up an office in the east wing fill it any equipment that you will need.

We will need to test not only her blood but mine as well and father I will need you to increase our security I am not taking any chances with Dillon's life.

Each vampire went about doing as they were instructed, Nicholas would let Dillon rest this night, but he would be at her door the first thing after he awakens the following night.

For now, Nicholas would descend down to the library to do some research but before he did, he instructed

166

Noah to ensure that he has a large quantity of blood on hand and to bring up a supply of his special homemade wine- blood mixture.

If he was going to have a house full of vampires and female humans in their midst, he needed to make sure that their temptations were as diminished as possible.

Dillon and Sarah decided to go to a day spa the next day and Sarah had planned for a couple of visits while they were on their vacation. They had not been able to enjoy their vacation at all but now they would at least try, and Sarah thought that a few spa days would help with Dillon's recovery.

Sarah noticed that Dillon was healing remarkably fast, which made her wonder if being with that vampire had affected Dillon.

Since it was true that vampires did seem to regenerate during their day sleep, maybe some of that healing power had transferred to Dillon and if it

The Vampire Romance Writer

is true that it had, what else could have been transferred?

These were Sarah's concerns, but Sarah dare not voice this to Dillon, she would wait until the time was right and now was not the right time.

After their spa day, they went to an early dinner then headed to Denver to meet Nicholas's father and try to figure their unique situation out.

Nicholas had asked that they come and spend a few days there so that they could try and figure out what was the connection they had between them.

Nicholas did not tell Dillon that he wanted her with him for her own safety.

Nicholas was relieved that Dillon had agreed relieved and even a little surprised.

168

The Vampire Romance Writer

Sarah was none too pleased to be in a house with one vampire but now that there was going to be another this really put her on edge and not to mention spending a night or two with them had her really freaked out.

On their drive to Denver Dillon noticed that Sarah was wearing a long scarf that she had wrapped around her neck as many times as she could, Dillon started to laugh, what's so funny? Sarah asked, well you and that scarf.

If a vampire wanted to suck on your neck that scarf would not stop him, well at least it might stop him from being tempted, they both laughed at that.

The drive to Denver took about an hour, Dillon had put the directions into the navigation system, it directed them to what could only be called a castle as they drove up to the manned gate they were stopped and informed that there were no visitors allowed.

The Vampire Romance Writer

You do not understand Dillon began, Nicholas Logan is expecting me, the guard came out of the gatehouse, frustration clearly evident in his voice.

You will have to leave, or you will be arrested, he told her in his stern voice.

Dillon saw that he had raised jacket back to show the gun he had holstered on his side.

By the time the guard had finished his sentence Nicholas was standing right behind him, excuse me this is Dillon Lane and I informed all the guards that she would be arriving.

Now can you please tell me why you are not letting her in and why are you treating her as she is some piece of trash that you can talk down to.

The guard looked as if he would die from fright; Nicholas looked as if he could kill him.

The Vampire Romance Writer

Dillon jumped out of the SUV and stood in between them, being careful not to touch Nicholas.

Please let's all just calm down I am sure that he must not have gotten the message, the guard was trying to explain that was what had happened, he had not received his oncoming report from the other guard as of yet.

Can we please go up to your house now? It is starting to get a little cold out here said Dillon trying to get Nicholas's attention off the guard.

Nicholas told her to drive straight up to the front door that he would be along shortly.

As Dillon drove away, she was praying that Nicholas would not hurt the poor guard; she would ask him as soon as he got back to his house.

The driveway led her around a large pound even in the dark she could tell that the property was enormous.

171

The Vampire Romance Writer

Dillon parked under the portico, as soon as she did there was a servant there to remove their bags and then he said he would park her vehicle for her.

Both ladies stood in awe looking up at the castle.

It was as if Dillon had just walked up to a castle in one of the fairy tales, she read as a child.

A butler greeted them and led them into a large room that Dillon assumed was the study with its grand fireplace and enough seating for a small army.

It was not a comfortable looking room, dark wood bookshelves lined each wall, each shelf packed full of books of every sort. Every chair was made of the same dark wood and covered in dark chocolate leather; large upholstered rugs were scattered over the dark wood floors the whole room was very masculine. A maid arrived and offered them something to drink both declined.

172

The Vampire Romance Writer

Sarah leaned over to Dillon as the maid was walking away, do you think that they would serve us blood?

Dillon cut her eyes at Sarah and shook her head at her; the maid motioned them to take a seat next to the grand fireplace. Nicholas had made sure that there was enough staff there to assist the ladies with whatever needs they might have.

To Dillon's surprise, she noticed Sarah seemed to be enjoying every minute of it.

It was a little while before Nicholas entered the study; may I give you a brief tour?

Eager to do something other than just sit the ladies jumped up and followed as Nicholas lead the way.

They were showed mainly the downstairs with one exception the east wing.

That side of the house he left for last this is where

The Vampire Romance Writer

Nicholas had an office set up equipment to assist in trying to determine what were Dillon's abilities, how and why they affected vampires.

As they entered the room, Dillon and Sarah thought that they had stepped into a doctor's office, but this office was just for one patient.

Nicholas asked if it would be all right if some blood was drawn and her temperature taken.

At first, Dillon started to say no, then nodded as she looked at Nicholas, he led her to a chair where a woman that Dillon knew was also a vampire just by her looks alone.

She was beautiful, and her skin had the same paleness to it, she looked like a living porcelain doll.

The lady vampire put on two pairs of long surgical gloves before withdrawing eight vials of Dillon's blood.

The Vampire Romance Writer

Dillon had another question to add to her list of questions that she would ask Nicholas.

How was it that they did not seem to want to attack them when they saw her blood?

Next Dillon's temperature was taken by a thermal body-imaging scanner that was set up in the corner of the room.

After what seemed like hours, they were led back down to the study.

Nicholas never left Dillon's side throughout the tour and testing. Always so, close but never touching even though his desire too was starting to get the better of him.

When they entered the study, Erick and Samuel were there, both vampires stood when they entered.

Dillon, Sarah, this my eternal father Erick and this is Samuel my lifelong friend he will be heading the testing for us.

175

Sarah reached out her hand and shook each vampire's hands. Dillon reached out hers, and then quickly withdrew forgetting that she would make them pass out.

Dillon thought that they should leave that maybe spending a couple of days here was not a good idea; she suddenly had the urge to call her daughters.

Dillon had not even thought of telling them about the "vampires" that they had met.

Dillon knew they would think her crazy as she herself was feeling now about the whole situation.

Dillon was hoping that Sarah would be as eager to leave as she was.

When Dillon suggested that, maybe they should be leaving and head back to Denver.

176

The Vampire Romance Writer

No was, shouted in Unisom from Sarah and Nicholas by
Dillon's suggestion. Dillon was not surprised by
Nicholas's response but she sure was by Sarah's.

I think we should stay and finish this testing they
may need to draw more blood or something. Maybe
Samuel would like to do an examination of you, and I
can assist him if he needs me too.

I think that is a good idea if you do not mind
Ms. Lane. Samuel responded, please call me Dillon,
all right, Dillon said as she gave Sarah a fleeting look.

Samuel led them back to the east wing, gave Dillon a
robe and showed her where to change. Dillon asked
that Sarah come with her, Sarah knew that
Dillon was upset that she postponed their leaving.

The Vampire Romance Writer

Chapter 20

As soon as she shut the door behind them Dillon turned to Sarah, are you crazy? Well, why did you change your mind and want to leave? Sarah asked. Why did you change your mind and want to stay, Asked Dillon?

We still have to be careful around vampires, said Dillon; hey, I am not the one sleeping with a vampire! Not yet anyway was Sarah's almost inaudible response.

You are not the only one that might want to date a vampire, I think that Samuel and I may have a connection too, or at least I would like there to be.

Dillon couldn't blame her, she knew how powerful the attraction to a vampire could be, just turn around so I can undress, Dillon left her underwear on she did

The Vampire Romance Writer

not fill comfortable to be completely naked, it would make her feel more vulnerable than she already did.

As they walked back into the office Nicholas was immediately at Dillon's side, as if he was her personal bodyguard.

Samuel motioned her to a table that looked more like a chiropractors table; she whispered to Nicholas what is he going to do adjust me? Samuel instructed her to slide off the robe and lay face down, she did as she was told, as Nicholas held up a sheet to give her some privacy, then he placed the sheet over her nearly bare rear.

Dillon watched as Samuel had put on a pair of surgical gloves the kind that goes up to your elbows and turned to Nicholas and asked his permission for him to examine Dillon, she and Nicholas both said yes. Dillon did not know why he asked Nicholas, but she had an idea, in their eyes she belonged to Nicholas.

Samuel first placed his gloved hands on her head, held them there for a couple of minutes then he slid them

179

The Vampire Romance Writer

to her armpits, again he did not move for a couple more minutes.

Samuel repeated the process all the way down her body but skipping over her pelvis.

Dillon sensed Nicholas trying to control his gut reaction to attack another vampire touching his woman.

When Samuel had finished, he told Dillon that she could get dressed, Dillon dressed as quickly as possible then returned to the others. Well, what do you think? Were the first words out of Dillon's mouth as she rejoined the others?

There are many unknown forces that cannot be explained in this world just as you did not know that vampires existed until a few days ago, I have never seen anyone affect vampires as you do, your body temperature is normal in the human sense when it is measured it is normal? Correct?

180

The Vampire Romance Writer

Yes! Dillon answered. But this is only my thoughts you must understand, just my initial assessment but when you come in contact with a vampire. You have a defense that no other person that we know of has; you can stop us in our track, just by your touch.

You make our blood warm and start to circulate through our body at a high rate of speed and the blood rushes to fast for our brains to compensate and we lose consciousness.

And as for being able to awaken a vampire from our sleep of renewal or day sleep as some call it, you were successfully able to awaken Nicholas, to that I would advise you to use caution. That area will need extensive research and testing. I do not know the purpose of your powers, but we need to find out and more importantly, we need to keep this a secret.

It would be dangerous for you if it got out that there's a way for a vampire to be awake in the daylight and even more dangerous than it may be

possible for you to turn a vampire back to human
again.

This is my conclusion from what I have been told by
Nicholas and from the simple test that I just did.

I could feel your heat through the gloves; it is as if
the heat wanted to jump from your body into mine.

I was able to see the glow of your heat like the heat
emitting from the sun. Even though your body
temperature is normal, it seems to transform somehow
when you are in close proximity to a vampire.

As Samuel explained his theory Sarah sat very still
trying to hang on to, his every word, Dillon knew that
Sarah was having a hard time understanding him
through his thick Louisiana accent, but Sarah got the
gist.

Dillon continued to listen to Samuel when Samuel was
finished Dillon did not know what to say. Dillon had

The Vampire Romance Writer

been thinking along the same lines as Samuel and she was just as concerned as he was.

Not about others finding out though but about her losing control and injuring Nicholas, being that she did not know anything about this so-called power that she has.

Dillon turned her attention to Sarah; "I think we should go" was Dillon's only response. I am sorry Dillon, but Samuel has asked me out to go out this evening and I have accepted.

Oh! Ok was all Dillon said? Dillon had to get away from all this; she needed to clear her head, she felt as though she was an animal trapped in a cage.

Dillon turned to Nicholas; I am going back to the cabin I think I made a mistake saying that I would stay. I am sorry can you please call for my bag and car? Dillon asked Nicholas.

We can talk later was all she said and turned to leave. Sarah and Nicholas both followed. Sarah turned

The Vampire Romance Writer

to Nicholas and asked for a moment alone with Dillon,
Nicholas agreed. Are you sure you're going to be ok?
Sarah asked, yes, I am fine I just need to think
things over clear my mind a little and I need to call
the girls, so you go and have a good time.

Dillon kissed Sarah on the cheek and turned to
Nicholas who was at her side in an instant. I need to
be alone for a while, please give me this time. Yes, of
course, I know this all must be overwhelming to you
as it would be for anyone who has just learned that
they possibly had the power to bring like back into a
being.

I want you to know that I am only staying away
because you asked; otherwise, I would not let you out
of my sight.

Dillon saw the hurt in Nicholas's eyes, but she had to
go and separate herself from all this, she just turned
and walked away.

184

The Vampire Romance Writer

After Dillon left Nicholas went straight to his father,
I will be gone until tomorrow night, there is no need
to worry, have them do every check that they can do
with what they have, yes, of course, Erick said, and
Nicholas was gone into the night.

Dillon needed to get out of there it was too much this
could not be real she had to be in one of her dreams;
she needed to wake up she thought.

Dillon reached the cabin, went straight to the
bedroom and called each of her daughters; she needed
to get a reality check.

After she finished speaking to her daughters, she
went into her bathroom to run her a hot bath, poured
in bubble bath and then stepped into the hot water.

Her mind was like a whirlwind; all she could think was
that she had to go home, had to escape this unreal
situation.

Even before Dillon finished her last thought, Nicholas
was standing there in her bathroom, you cannot go; I

185

The Vampire Romance Writer

can't live without you. What are you a mind reader? To all people except for you, I cannot read yours but that does not mean I do not know what you are thinking I could see it on your face before you left my house earlier.

Please leave was all that she said. She honestly did not want him there at that moment. However, he would not go, please get out of the tub. We need to talk.

Dillon would not be told what to do; no, I will not, I asked you to please give me a little time to think things through. He looked her straight in the eyes, Dillon get out of the tub! Please!

Dillon knew that that was a command, and, in some tales, vampires could control you to some extent.

Dillon did not move; listen your mind control will not work on me and I will stay in until the water turns ice cold if I choose.

186

The Vampire Romance Writer

Now, this had never happened to him before, he could always get a woman to do whatever it was that he wanted her to do. Nicholas walked out to the bedroom and sat down and waited for her, he would wait for her until there was no trace of life left in his undead body.

Dillon took longer than usual but she could not stand being in there any longer, she wanted to run to him as much as she wanted to run from him, but she barely knew him and what little she did know was all so unbelievable.

If Dillon had not experienced this supernatural romance, herself she would not in a million years believed it.

Dillon knew Nicholas did not leave she had the feeling that he would ever leave her. Dillon could sense that he was just outside the bathroom door waiting, just waiting.

He had all the time in the world since he would never die; unless someone who should not exist came along

The Vampire Romance Writer

with the power to either make him human again or kill him someone like me.... she thought.

Dillon dressed in her pajamas and went to the bedroom.

Dillon found him just sitting there, Dillon had the feeling that he could still kill her in an instant whether she had this power or not. No one did not really know for sure what this power was, or even where it came from.

Still, she did not fear him; Dillon knew she should with him being what most would call a monster.

What she felt for him though was love, a love so deep and pure that she felt consumed by it.

I cannot leave you; I will never leave you I have to stay by your side.

These were Nicholas's words that broke the silence between them. I have never felt like this with another

188

woman before and no woman has ever been able to calm me as you do.

I am unstable and uncontrollable when I am extremely upset like I am now with the thought of you walking out of my life and I have found that the only thing that keeps me calm is being with you.

What in the hell! Did you do before you met me? Dillon did not care what he thought, Dillon walked past him to her bed and laid down and watched her vampire just sit and guard over her. After a few minutes she motioned for him to lie beside her, I am going to sleep if you want to stay you can I have blocked the windows from the sun, so you should be all right, Dillon told him as she got under the covers and turned to go to sleep.

It did not take long for Dillon to fall asleep; she slept the night through; She did not dream a single dream that night.

Dillon did not think that she had even moved at all that night. When Dillon woke up, she had forgotten

189

The Vampire Romance Writer

that Nicholas was there as she turned over and saw him lying there, she jumped out of the bed then she remembered, she looked over at the clock seven-thirty, Nicholas was in a deep deathly sleep.

Dillon carefully opened the door making sure no sunlight could get in then closed the door quickly behind her; she crept quietly downstairs.

Dillon found Sarah sitting at the table drinking coffee, so how was your night? Dillon asked Sarah, it went unexpectedly well he took me out to dinner at a sushi restaurant then we went dancing and it has not been long since I got back.

How about you? Well not as exciting as yours I was just wanted to be alone, but Nicholas was not having that, yeah Samuel said that he was upstairs with you; they must be able to sense one another.

Yeah, he is fast asleep now. Well, I scheduled our second spa day for today we are to be there soon so

The Vampire Romance Writer

go and get dressed so that we can be on our way Sarah told Dillon.

We are to have lunch there also so please hurry so that we will not be late. Dillon did not protest what else she could do while her vampire was sleeping, so Dillon did as she was told and went to her room to dress being careful not to let in any sunlight as she opened the door leading to her room.

Nicholas was still fast asleep looking as though he was dead so lifeless, she thought.

Dillon leaned over and spoke quietly into his ear, can you tell me why? Why? Is it that I love you?

She stood up and just looked at him for a few seconds longer then left him there sleeping as she went to change clothes then headed back downstairs and within a few minutes, they were out the door on their way.

When they first arrived, they requested to have a mud bath, which they both agreed was not that bad.

The Vampire Romance Writer

After they had their nails and hair done then they went to have brunch. Well if we are going to date, vampires we should get used to eating alone Sarah said, as they sat down at their table. Dillon nodded and then asked what do you think about this whole vampire situation anyway?

Does it all seem as unreal to you as it does to me? Yes, Sarah agreed, Dillon continued and what about this ability that I can bring life back into vampire's completely unbelievable right?

Did you ever have any idea that you had any such powers?

How I could? I did not think that vampires were real let alone that I could bring life back into them.

You never sensed anything? Well, I knew that I had an intolerance to heat due to that fact that I was already hot-blooded you know what I mean I overheated easily. I would get heat sick if I stayed in

The Vampire Romance Writer

the sun too long, I never liked to turn on any heat, things like that, but that stuff ran in my family.

Well now we know that it was more than heat intolerance, you have a gift that had to be given to you for a reason.

You did tell me that your grandfather was a Cherokee Indian maybe that was something that was passed down to you to help the vampires that did not want to remain a vampire change back to a human.

Dillon thought for a moment you know what? We are two brilliant women I think that you may be on to something there we need to do further research on it. Maybe we could ask Samuel, see what he thinks Sarah liked the idea she would have another reason to see Samuel again.

When they got home, Dillon went up to check on Nicholas, he was still in his deathly sleep, truly frozen like the dead that she had seen many times in her life the same cold lifeless skin, void of color, his body unable to move.

193

The Vampire Romance Writer

When Dillon truly thought about the concept that Nicholas was really a vampire, she knew that when she was faced with such evidence as what was right in front of her there was no denying what he was.

The Vampire Romance Writer

Chapter 21

Dillon could not take it any longer her desire for him was overwhelming she did not heed the warning to not be awakening him during his day sleep. Dillon needed to be with him she could not wait any longer.

Dillon dressed in nothing but a pink sheer robe and went to retrieve her smelling salts, Dillon walked to his side she laid her hands on his chest when she did, she felt him jump from the shock of her warmth or something else she could not say.

Dillon lightly rubbed her fingers over his chest letting her touch warm his blood slowly as she did, she noticed his muscles they were solid she wondered if this was a contributing factor in his tremendous strength.

When she thought that she had warmed his blood and sped his heart up enough Dillon placed the smelling salts once again under his nose and again it took a while before he began to stir. When he did awaken,

195

Nicholas automatically reached for her and began kissing her, his kisses were so fierce and overpowering that Dillon felt as though he was trying to suck the life out of her.

Dillon tried to pull away, but Nicholas would not let her go. He continued to kiss her, but he loosened up slightly.

Nicholas had forgotten that she was human. Nicholas let his lips slide from her mouth down to her neck. Oh, how he would love to sink his teeth into her Nicholas thought but he knew he had to resist he did not want to totally lose control as he knew he could very easily do so.

Instead, he turned her over, rose above her, and started kissing her from head to toe. When he could not take it anymore Nicholas crawled back up to her and began kissing her deeply once again just before he slid into her feeling her heat envelope him from the inside as well as out.

196

The Vampire Romance Writer

Her kisses were filled with life and energy when he kissed her, he felt alive; Nicholas felt a deep inner need to drink from her a need so strong like none before.

Somewhere deep inside something was telling him that this was what he was supposed to do, drink from her let her give him her lifeblood, blood that would in turn somehow fill him with life. Her blood seemed to be calling out for him to consume it, to take from her, what was truly meant to be his.

Nicholas let his lips slide from hers, down to her neck; Nicholas could hear the blood rushing through her jugular as Dillon whispered for him to drink from her.

Dillon wanted him to drink from her, wanted her life force to flow into him, wanted him to consume her blood so that it would become part of him.

Dillon was begging him to drink from her. Nicholas was trying to resist Dillon's pleas and the voice deep inside him as well. Please! Please! Dillon whispered,

The Vampire Romance Writer

finally Nicholas sank his teeth into her neck and began to drink as he did, he felt the hot liquid

spilling down his throat, he never tasted any blood like hers before it seemed electrified with life.

Nicholas continued to drink, then he came to the height of his orgasm he suddenly felt as though his whole body had an electric shock, he had to let go of her he could not hold on any longer.

Nicholas's body began to tremble and a wave of what could only be nausea swept over him, Nicholas lay down beside Dillon. Dillon could tell that something was not right; she was terrified wondering what she may have done to him this time.

What is wrong? Dillon asked him, I do not know Nicholas answered honesty.

Nicholas had not thrown up since he was human. Nevertheless, that was the way he was feeling right

The Vampire Romance Writer

now, as though he could empty his stomach until
there was nothing left inside him.

Suddenly Nicholas could not hold back any longer he
jumped from the bed, just making it to the bathroom
in time before he started throwing up.

However, it was not her blood that he threw up it was
just clear liquid. After Nicholas emptied, his stomach
of its contents he freshened up, he returned to her
side.

Are you ok? Dillon asked I think I am now, what is
happening?

I do not know I just know that that has not happened
to me since I was human. Did my blood make you
sick? No, I don't think so not the blood itself, I
think I had a reaction to what is in your blood.

I am sorry that I begged you to drink from me it just
seemed the right thing to do it was as if something
deep inside of me was saying tell him to drink from

you and when you did it was the best feeling that I have ever experienced.

Nicholas never mentioned to Dillon that he had the same feeling as something was beckoning him to drink from her.

Dillon laid her head on his chest again and he wrapped his arms around her, she was oblivious to the slight increase in his body temperature.

Nicholas lifted her chin and kissed her softly on the lips, listen I am fine just a little shock to my system that is all, so please do not worry.

Soon after his kisses turned back into the fierce ones as before and once again, he was inside her and once again, Dillon was pleading for him to drink, drink until his heart's content and as before, he did her bidding.

The electricity was magnified this time and the nausea returned more intense than before. It swept over him in waves, it all ended in an electrified orgasmic

200

explosion inside of him and Nicholas again just made it to the bathroom before he began to throw up, violently this time.

When Nicholas finally finished, he found Dillon by his side, looking at him with concern on her face. I am fine, but we must find out what is happening to me when I drink your blood, and until we do, I cannot do it again.

We cannot take any more reckless chances with this power you have; Dillon nodded her head in agreement.

Dillon filled the tub with hot water; a hot bath would do them both good she thought.

Nicholas stepped in Dillon followed sitting down in front of Nicholas. As they sat there, Dillon in Nicholas' arms, Dillon's thoughts lingered on what had just happened to Nicholas, she wondered how is it that she could possess such power and not know that she had it.

The Vampire Romance Writer

There had to be a reason that this power was surfacing now, why not any other time in her life.

If vampires are truly real and she had to admit that they were, she was bathing with one at this very moment, then she most certainly would have met one in passing at some point in her life. Why then did none who met her never notice this power? Dillon did not voice any of her thoughts or concerns to Nicholas.

They lingered in the tub until the water started to turn cold. Dillon climbed from the tub Nicholas followed behind her. Dillon could tell that he still needed his sleep even though now it was late afternoon.

I think that you should try to sleep, Dillon told him, but Nicholas started to protest I don't feel as if I need too, Dillon knew that he was trying to stay awake more for her benefit than his.

The Vampire Romance Writer

Dillon took him by the hand and led him to her bed where they both laid down and eventually fell asleep.

Dillon woke up after only a couple hours' sleep; she lay there for a few minutes just watching him.

Nicholas seemed so peaceful, he did seem to have a little more color to him, Dillon placed her hand lightly on his arm he was still cold but not as much as before.

Dillon had a fleeting thought could her warmth combined with her blood was turning back into a human or was it poisoning him?

Dillon slipped out of bed and headed downstairs where she knew Sarah be waiting, she had to run her thoughts by Sarah and see if any of them made any sense.

Dillon and Sarah spent the rest of the evening discussing what had happened to Nicholas, Dillon told Sarah of her thoughts on what her touch and blood

203

The Vampire Romance Writer

may do to Nicholas neither one could come up with any answers, just more questions.

The Vampire Romance Writer

Chapter 22

By the time, the Sun had set Dillon and Sarah were all ready to go to Nicholas's house, Dillon went up just as Nicholas was rising, how do you feel? She asked I feel fine, no nausea, nothing. Maybe we should run some tests on you as well, Nicholas agreed.

Sarah and I are ready to leave for your house if that is where you want to go this evening.

That is exactly where I want to go; I would like to see if there are any results on the tests performed on you.

As they were pulling into Nicholas's driveway Nicholas sensed a new guest at his house, a guest he would usually be delighted to see but this was not the time or the placed to introduce the woman he had waited his entire life for to his mother!

Dillon could tell that Nicholas's demeanor had changed as soon as they approached his house but

The Vampire Romance Writer

why she could not tell but as they walked into the study, she got her answer.

Everyone was gathered in the study but tonight there was a new face in the crowd of Vampires.

A beautiful woman with long straight black hair and the same jet-black eyes as Nicholas, she looked as though she was a princess.

An American Indian princess at that. Mother? Nicholas cried, what are you doing here?

"Oh my God! Oh my God! Was what going through

Dillon's mind, Nicholas saw the expression on Dillon's face and quickly whispered to her, calm down it will be ok.

Nicholas went straight to his mother, she grabbed her son and embraced him tightly then Nicholas started to make the introductions but before he could, Sable walked over to Dillon.

The Vampire Romance Writer

I would shake your hand, but I have been advised not to. Nice to meet your mam, was all Dillon could get out.

Sarah reached out her hand and the two women shook hands then Sable turned back to
look at Dillon I see her aura it is bright white it is the strongest that I have seen, she was speaking to Nicholas, as though Dillon was an inanimate object.

Thankfully Erick cut in, Sable let the woman be, please everyone has a seat.

Dillon did not want to sit she wanted to go to the office and see any results that may be ready, Samuel could we go and check if there are any results on the tests.

Dillon asked, yes, of course, then he led the way as Dillon and Sarah followed. Dillon did not want to stand there and be subjected to any more of Sable's examination of her.

The Vampire Romance Writer

On the way there, Samuel could tell that Dillon wanted to talk about something other than her special abilities, but he waited until they were behind closed doors before asking, he led Dillon and Sarah over to a table and they all sat down.

Before we start, I feel that you have other information that you would like to share.

Dillon was starting to get used to how perceptive that vampires were. Yes, there is a lot that I need to talk to you about then she proceeded to tell him about Nicholas, and she suggested that he also run some tests on him.

Samuel seemed worried about the information, but he proceeded to tell her that the preliminary results showed nothing out of the ordinary her body scanned did show increased thermal spikes but nothing else.

I figured as much though I think your abilities run deeper that the tests that we have run, we have been

The Vampire Romance Writer

testing you on what we consider the natural realm I think we should test you on the unnatural or supernatural so to speak.

Dillon and Sarah both were thinking the same thing; how would you test for supernatural powers.

Soon Nicholas joined them and after he was given the results of Dillon's tests, Nicholas agreed to have some test ran on him also.

Samuel collected a couple of glass vials and started to draw Nicholas's blood.

Dillon and Sarah both observed the vial as it filled slowly with blood. The blood seemed much darker to Dillon than human blood, but she supposed that since vampires were dead that their blood would be darker since they barely breathed and in turn would not have much oxygen in it.

Samuel finished drawing the blood both vampires were examining the vials, does it look brighter than it should be, fresher? Samuel asked Nicholas; let us do a thermal scan on you to see if there are any changes there.

Dillon just listen to what the vampires were discussing if his blood looked brighter than usual what did it look like before?

When they were finished with all the testing, they all went back down to the study.

As they entered the room Dillon could feel Sable's eyes upon her, she had the feeling that Nicholas mother did not approve of her at all.

Sable was sitting close to her husband, Dillon wondered if the mother-son connection also occurred in the vampire realm and if it did, she would be willing to bet that it was much, much stronger than the human mother-son connection.

Dillon pulled Sarah to the side, we have to get out of here, I cannot be here any longer, she nodded her

The Vampire Romance Writer

head toward Sable, Sarah agreed and went to say goodnight to Samuel.

Dillon had the feeling that Sarah was okay with being in a house with one or two vampires but being in a house overflowing with them had her as eager to leave as Dillon was.

Dillon told Nicholas that they were leaving, he, of course, did not want her to go but she insisted, then he said that he would go with her.

Dillon was determined to go alone this time just her and Sarah and let Nicholas have this time be alone with his parents.

To Dillon's surprise, he did not protest but agreed but only with the understanding that he would be around to see her sometime before dawn.

Nicholas walked the women to their car and as Dillon was saying good-bye to Nicholas, she forgot that she could not touch him after dark and leaned forward to hug him. Dillon suddenly remembered this, but it was too late.

Nicholas went down onto his knees as soon as he felt her touch by the time Dillon could bend down to check on him Sable was at her side.

Dillon felt herself being hit with something that sent her flying across the yard landing so hard that she felt that most of her bones had to have broken with the force not only from whatever she was hit with but also with her impact with the ground.

Sarah rushed to Dillon's side Dillon was struggling to catch her breath since the impact with the ground also knocked the breath from her.

Dillon! Dillon! Are you alright? Dillon could hear Sarah but was unable to inhale any air into her lungs to breath let alone answer.

212

The Vampire Romance Writer

It took only a few seconds for her lungs to be able to expand so that she could breathe but it seemed like an eternity to Dillon.

Sarah sat by Dillon's side checking her for injuries, thankful that she found none, but she could tell that Dillon was dazed but she seemed to be coming around.

Dillon are you ok. Can you sit up? Sarah was trying to get Dillon to respond, Dillon finally nodded her head.

Sarah helped her to sit up.

Dillon sat there a couple of minutes longer until her head cleared and was able to focus her mind on what just happened, suddenly it hit her. Dillon got up and ran to where Sable was kneeling by Nicholas.

Dillon felt as if her blood was boiling and the desire to kill Sable so strong, she had never wanted to hurt someone like she wanted to now.

However, as she drew, back to hit Sable Dillon found herself restrained by Noah and the butler, let me go! Dillon screamed but they would not, they tried to calm her and reminded her that she was no match for a vampire that did no good she was becoming more furious with each passing second.

Sarah was demanding that they let her go, we cannot, and Dillon will be killed if she attacks Mrs. Logan.

Dillon, please calm down Sarah was saying to her, but Dillon's concentration was on trying to get out of the death grip that the men had on her.

Dillon focused all her attention on trying to get to Sable that she did not notice that Nicholas was only stunned by her touch. Erick and Samuel were assisting him to his feet and leading him into his house.

Dillon was led to her car as Sarah rushed and got in the drivers' seat the two men were trying to force Dillon into the passenger's seat, finally they got the

The Vampire Romance Writer

door shut. Sarah drove off as fast as she could while trying to keep Dillon from jumping from the moving car.

What were you thinking Dillon? You know that you cannot win a battle with a vampire, but I can die trying was Dillon's only reply. Dillon calmed down on the drive back to their rented cabin; her mind was racing, still feeling the rush that the adrenaline gave her so many thoughts were running through her head, but she came to a firm decision.

Dillon needed to get as far away from those damn vampires as she could.

Sarah, I need to get away from here tonight, we need to go before Nicholas regains his strength, where will we go? We still have the cabin. We will be back I need a break, time to think and I cannot do that when I am around Nicholas. They drove back to the cabin, packed a few items, and headed out.

The Vampire Romance Writer

Chapter 23

Nicholas was lying in his bed still weak but as he managed to sit up, he noticed his mother at his bedside, mother where is Dillon? Were the first words he uttered; son you need your rest we can talk later you are not well.

I do not know what powers she holds within her, but those powers are dangerous as evidence in her ability to bring down one of the strongest vampires that I have ever known with the slightest touch.

Nicholas paid her no mind he was determined to see Dillon but as he stood up the room started to spin, and he was enveloped in total darkness.

Sable ran to him catching him before he hit the floor, she called for Erick he came running in they quickly assisted him back to bed. Erick, what is going on?

216

The Vampire Romance Writer

We are not exactly sure what his being in contact with Dillon is doing to him or how it is, being done Erick replied.

How can we help him? When we do not know anything about this woman's powers and what she is capable of for all we know she is trying to destroy us all.

Samuel came in and tried to calm Sable down, he will be fine he just needs to rest he is going through some changes; his body just needs to adjust.

Changes? What kind of changes? You need to tell me what this woman is doing to my son?

Please sit-down Sable, from all the tests that we have done so far, all that we really know is that her touch can stop a vampire in his or her tracks and that her blood does seem to have some regeneration properties to it but other than that we are totally in the dark so to speak.

So please let your son rest and I think he will be good as new this evening, but I don't think that when

217

he wakes, he will be too happy that you attacked his future wife.

Sable would not leave Nicholas's side until almost dawn when she did, it was only to turn in for the day but before joining her husband in their quarters, she gave strict instructions to Noah to watch over Nicholas during the day and not to let Dillon near him.

Nicholas woke before the sunset; this had never happened to him before and he had never heard of it happening to another vampire either.

Nicholas was starving he rang for a couple of bottles of his special wine and the maid came within minutes followed by Noah, sir you are up already? Apparently so, was Nicholas's reply how it that possible? Nicholas ignored him, where are my parents? Still asleep sir.

I need to talk to Sable as soon as she is awake also can you please get my cell; I have got a lot of apologizing to do and so does Sable.

218

The Vampire Romance Writer

Nicholas had seen what his mother had done to Dillon and how Dillon tried her best to return the favor, Nicholas knew that Dillon did not mean intentionally harm him.

Noah left to get Nicholas's cell while he waited Nicholas drank a whole bottle of wine then started on another. Noah returned with Nicholas's cell; Nicholas quickly dialed Dillon's number it went straight to voice mail. Nicholas then dialed Sarah's phone it also went to the voice mail.

Nicholas jumped up, have my car brought around he told Noah, then dressed quickly and was down before the car was ready.

Sir, it is not dark yet, Nicholas paid him no mind and rushed to his car so fast that all you could see was a blur.

Nicholas had a feeling that the setting sun would not harm him, and he was right.

The Vampire Romance Writer

Nicholas drove almost as fast as he ran to his car; he arrived at the cabin and immediately knew that she was gone.

Nicholas was in her room in the blink of an eye he saw that some of her things were missing; he suddenly felt himself being overcome with emotion.

He dropped to his knees and began to cry, he sobbed so hard that he felt as if his insides were being ripped apart, then the tears came like a fountain running down his cheeks he did not know or care what was happening to him.

All that he knew was that he loved her, and she was gone, gone out of his life.

Nicholas remained like this for what seemed like hours before he was able to compose himself when he did, he called Samuel to see if had any idea as to where they were, he did not of course.

220

The Vampire Romance Writer

Nicholas rushed back to his house and ran straight to Sable, you did this! You made her leave he grabbed her and threw her across the room before anyone had a chance to stop him and when they did it took both Samuel and Erick, even with their combined strength it was a challenge to pull him from her.

Sable stood up walked slowly to where her son was.

Sable spoke to Nicholas as if he were a child, it is for your own good that she has gone, she is slowly destroying you and you don't even care. You think that the mortal has the power to make you live again, the only power she has is to kill you and to make you turn on your family.

What I do with my life is none of your business and if I chose to die, at least I will die happy with the woman that I love and that truly loves me.

Love? You do not know what that is, you had it in your grasp at one time when you promised yourself to Jade and look how that ended up. You betrayed her by breaking the sacred bond of vampire marriage; you know that if we marry then we do so for life.

Yes, mother that is if the woman that you are supposed to love forever truly loves you but her only motive was only to destroy me.

Sable did not know what to say, she had always loved Jade, and she never forgave Nicholas for breaking up their marriage.

You never listened when I tried to talk to you concerning the reasons behind why I ended it with her, you just worried about the sacred bond of the vampire union.

Erick and Samuel finally released Nicholas seeing that he had calmed down Nicholas went straight to his quarters, called for his blood- wine mixture and red wine and before the sun rose, he had drunk two bottles of each.

Before turning in for the day Nicholas had given instructions to Noah to do his best to find Dillon before he rose that evening Noah promised he would do his best.

Dillon and Sarah drove to the only city close enough to get lost in, Las Vegas!

Dillon was hoping that the abundance of people would be a distraction on Nicholas's vampire senses. Dillon knew that Nicholas could not read her thoughts, but he could read everyone else is Sarah included, she was hoping that she could hide herself in the sea of humans.

When Nicholas rose, it was after sunset this time, Noah was eager to speak to him as soon as Nicholas called for him, Noah entered the room I have found her sir they are in Las Vegas!

Noah have my jet ready within the hour, it already is sir.

The Vampire Romance Writer

Nicholas showered and was out the door within minutes
Noah was waiting by his car along with Samuel, good
luck sir said Noah. I am going with you there is a
woman there that I love also, Samuel said, then let's
go and by the way Noah give yourself a raise,
Nicholas shouted as they drove away.

The flight seemed to take much longer than it
actually did but they made it there in no time.

The vampires went straight to their waiting car and to
the hotel where Dillon and Sarah were staying. They
used their keen senses and easily found them they
were having supper in the hotel restaurant.

When Nicholas saw Dillon, he was suddenly filled with
a mixture of joy, hurt, anger and love.

Nicholas never understood how someone could say that
they could feel all those feelings at the same time
until now.

224

The Vampire Romance Writer

Even before Dillon saw Nicholas, she could feel his presence; her eyes scanned the entire restaurant stopping at the entrance to the restaurant.

There he was Mr. Tall Dark and Handsome standing at the entrance staring at her with those piercing black eyes, she watched as he walked to where she and Sarah were sitting and just stood there beside her not saying a word.

Dillon knew that it would not take long for him to find her, but she did not think it would be that fast.

Nicholas wanted to grab her and squeeze the life out of her, but he just sat down beside her.

Neither said a word for a long time when Nicholas did speak all he said was why did you leave? Dillon did not answer did not even acknowledge that she even heard him.

Dillon just stared straight ahead not even turning to look at him she could see that she had hurt him deeply, could hear it in his voice.

The Vampire Romance Writer

Samuel and Sarah were paying no mind to either of them; they excuse themselves and left Dillon and Nicholas sitting there alone.

Dillon rose to leave, and Nicholas followed right behind. Nicholas did not know what to do but follow her as he walked behind her, he felt like a stray puppy, he was thinking how could a woman do this to me?

Literally, bring me to my knees, and take my heart and wrap her hand around it and make it feel as though it was being ripped out of my chest.

Love he thought true and everlasting love. Back in her room, Nicholas broke the silence and fell to his knees how could you put me through this?

Do you not know by now how much I love you; I have never loved anyone as I love you. The pain-filled him, a gut retching pain as this pain welled up in him it finally found an outlet, an outlet in his tears.

226

The Vampire Romance Writer

Nicholas was so overcome with this pain that he paid no attention to the fact that he had not shed tears since he was human, but this was the second time in as many days.

Dillon did not say a word what could she say, she loved him too but how was this going to work they were from two very different worlds.

Dillon walked over to the bed and sat down, still not saying a word, what was she to do?

Here she was in Las Vegas with a vampire pouring his heart out to her, she should be feeling as though she was the happiest woman on earth, wasn't this what she wanted?

True everlasting love, but she felt empty, she felt void of all feelings at that moment the only thing that she knew for sure was that she wanted to go home.

Dillon wanted to go back to her life, the life where she was alone when she really thought about it, she liked being alone. Dillon wanted her uncomplicated life

227

The Vampire Romance Writer

back, sure, it was a lonely life but at least it was her own.

This is why she did not like relationships they were a rollercoaster ride, one-minute things were the best that you could ever wish for then the next you're at the end of your rope trying to hang on for dear life wondering if you should let go and fall into the abyss below.

Oh, how she wished that she were in one of her dreams, one of her nightmares right now.

Dillon closed her eyes and just sat there thinking to herself, wake up Dillon, wake up but of course, she knew that would not work for she was awake and living her dream, her nightmare.

Nicholas continued to pour out his love for her, Dillon just sat there listening, listening but trying not to.

Dillon wanted to block out any feelings but instead of blocking her feeling, she felt as though she was about 228

The Vampire Romance Writer

to explode from the pressure that was building to the boiling point and then she started to cry.

Dillon's tears turned into an uncontrollable hysterical cry, his heartfelt as though it was bleeding, bleeding for her, he wanted so much to hold her, comfort her but how, how could he?

Leave! Dillon demanded leave just leave me alone! Dillon shouted my life was so much easier without you in it.

I don't want this kind of life, this is why I chose to be alone, I never wanted to feel like this again I want you to forget about me and I will do my best to forget about you.

I do not want to see you again ever. Dillon repeated over and over, this is not the life for me; this is not the life for me.

Nicholas got up he started to say something but just nodded and left her sitting there crying.

The Vampire Romance Writer

Dillon never even turned her head as he left; she just let him walk out into the night and out of her life.

The Vampire Romance Writer

Chapter 24

After Nicholas had gone Dillon let the floodwaters break from their gate, Dillon was shaking so violently and sobbing so deeply that she thought that she was dying.

Dillon continued like this until she made herself literally sick from sadness, she bolted to the bathroom and heaved until nothing was left inside her, she grabbed a towel and balled herself up on the floor and lay there crying eventually falling asleep on the cold bathroom floor.

Nicholas was enraged to the point that he could not control himself; he needed to get away from her from all humans before he took out his rage on an unsuspecting innocent human. Nicholas jumped into his car and headed for the desert how could she deny him?

How could she dismiss him as a servant? Had he been mistaken about her being his soul mate? The one he had searched for. Longed for?

All these questions ran through his mind as he sped toward the desert, to the nothingness that he sought he should just sit in the desert and let the sunrise and incinerate him then his heart would hurt no more.

With this last thought, Nicholas found what he was trying to avoid, she was walking on the outskirts of town, he pulled up to her, grabbed her before she knew what happened.

Nicholas tore into her neck, drank until she was almost dead before he stopped, then he let her near lifeless body fall to the ground. Nicholas disappeared into the night, still delirious with the rage that was inside him.

Nicholas had tried his best to leave but he found himself heading back to the hotel back to Dillon.

The Vampire Romance Writer

Nicholas had spent the night trying his best to escape the torcher that enveloped him from the fear of losing her, but he realized that there was no future without her.

When Nicholas arrived at the hotel, he found Dillon lying on the bathroom floor asleep. Nicholas let her lay there as he went and showered. Nicholas needed to get the scent of the woman that he nearly killed off him.

After he showered, Nicholas decided that he would carry Dillon to her bed and lay beside her and if he passed out then at least he would be unconscious with her in his arms.

He grabbed a blanket and wrapped her in it trying his best to will her not to awaken, not knowing if it would work but she did not stir as he carried her to the bed.

Nicholas eased her down onto the bed and lay alongside her careful not to touch her until he was ready.

233

The Vampire Romance Writer

Nicholas hovered his arm over her then as he kissed her neck, he lowered his arm down over her, almost immediately he started to feel faint but did not lose consciousness immediately but slowly the darkness surrounded him.

When Dillon woke, she felt Nicholas's arms around her, Dillon breathed in the unmistakable scent that she knew was Nicholas and that made her feel at peace.

Dillon knew that he must have returned during the night and carried her to bed, she turned over and looked at him, she did love him, this she knew, loved him so much it hurt but as she found out the night before, losing him would most certainly lead to her demise.

Dillon leaned forward and kissed him softly on the lips then on his neck, she could hear his heart speed up

234

with each kiss. Dillon reluctantly pulled away and let her vampire sleep.

Dillon walked into the bathroom stood in in front of the mirror, she looked tired, so tired, she thought to herself aren't you supposed to be refreshed when you go on vacation.

Dillon turned from her reflection, went, and ran the tub full of hot water and bubbles then sank deep into the water after her relaxing soak she dressed and headed downstairs for something to eat.

When she got to the restaurant, she found Sarah already there, hello Dillon Sarah said, where you have been.

Dillon asked Sarah. Where do you think? I have been with Samuel, he is resting now, Dillon did not say anything to Sarah about the big bite mark she saw on Sarah's neck, well let's get something to eat while the vampires sleep.

The Vampire Romance Writer

When they finished eating, they walked around the casino, talking over what they were going to do.

I am going to go away with Samuel for a while after he has finished his business with Nicholas and if it works out then I will decide if I want to make it permanent.

Dillon knew what she meant by business, she knew that the business was she, and as for her making her relationship permanent, Dillon knew that Sarah meant being transformed into a vampire.

Dillon could not blame Sarah for wanting to prolong her life at this late stage in her life Sarah was in her sixties, but she could easily pass for Dillon's age.

The years seem to go by faster as you get older, it would be hard to pass up eternal life even if you are in vampire form.

236

Dillon told her that she would stand by whatever choice she made. Sarah asked what Dillon was going to do.

Dillon told her truthfully that she did not know she went on to tell her what happened the night before.

Sarah told her that Samuel had said that Nicholas lost it after they left Nicholas's house that night and that Samuel had never seen him so mad before, he actually had a confrontation with his mother and that was a first.

After they finished their tour of the hotel-casino, they decided to go do a little sightseeing and shopping and try to put a little normalcy in their day.

Their site seeing lasted into the late afternoon, throughout the day Dillon could not shake the feeling of being watched.

Dillon the same feeling she had not that long ago, she knew that before that it was Nicholas who watched

The Vampire Romance Writer

her, she almost expected to see him around each corner she turned but of course, she did not.

After they walked all that their legs could stand, they decided to return to the hotel.

Dillon walked Sarah to her room, and then Dillon went back to hers. She still did not know what to do about Nicholas, she knew she loved him, loved him more than she had loved any man.

Dillon sat down and watched him sleep; he was such a beautiful specimen, perfect in every way.

He was the type of man that any woman would die to be with, she had never seen anyone like him before but here she was questioning what she should do.

Dillon had no doubt that he loved her, but love is not always enough.

Sitting there waiting on him to awaken Dillon's desire to be with him increased with each passing moment.

238

Dillon could not take it any longer she had to be with him, if Dillon did not awaken him now, he would not be able to withstand her touch when he awoke on his own.

Dillon went into her bag grabbed her spirit of hartshorn and returned to her bed. Dillon leaned over him and gently placed her hands on his chest and just as before she immediately noticed his heart rate speed up.

Dillon placed the spirit of hartshorn under his nose he started slowly coming around, when he was fully awake Nicholas quickly turned to her, grabbed her and began kissing her fiercely.

Don't ever tell me to leave again, those were the first words out of his mouth I will die if you do.

I not only want to be with you I need to be with you I know now that I literally can't live without you nor would I want to live in this world without you.

The Vampire Romance Writer

Dillon laid her head on his shoulder; put her arms around him, not saying a word, for no words were necessary her actions were enough.

Nicholas pulled her closer to him and kissed her softly. Nicholas could feel the energy flow from her body to his, a slight tingling sensation that seemed to spread to every cell in his body he could feel life flowing back into his body.

He did not feel that he was becoming human again but there was no mistaken life was once again budding inside of him.

After a few moments Dillon finally spoke up, she wanted answers to her many questions, she thought now would be as good a time as any to ask those questions.

How did you become a vampire? And how long have you been a vampire?

240

The Vampire Romance Writer

Nicholas had never shared details about how he had become a vampire with another soul before; he was even now reluctant to tell Dillon.

Nicholas felt compelled to tell her, it was as if she had a spell on him, a spell to tell her anything that she wanted to know.

His story started to pour out of him as if he had no control over his own words.

I was born into vampirism out of desperation, a desperation to kill every vampire that I met.

I was a warrior before I was a vampire and when I was gone to battle my whole family was slaughtered for food by a band of vampires that had no compassion for human life.

I spent several years looking for a vampire who would turn me; this was not an easy task.

The Vampire Romance Writer

You cannot go around asking if someone is a vampire and then follow up by asking him to turn you into one.

I watched, waited, and learned, learned how to tell a vampire from a human.

Finally, some years later I found Erick he could read my thoughts and found out my reasons for wanting to be a vampire. He hesitated for a few weeks then suddenly one day he agreed. Did he ever tell you why he agreed, knowing your reasons for wanting to be a vampire?

No, he never told me, and I never asked not even to this day.

I enjoyed being a vampire I love the power it gave me not just the physical power but also the power to control humans.

I treasured this power the most.

242

The physical power that I had, as a human seemed to increase a hundred-fold.

My new ability to control people was most enjoyable, not all were easy to control the ones that we're able to resist me well I found pleasure in those as well.

I loved the thrill of the fight, the more they resisted the harder I tried. Eventually, my mind overtook theirs and they did my bidding mostly to serve my need for blood.

I did not always kill them, but I did leave most to die. I was blessed with the ability to read human and vampires minds, a trait that not well known in the vampire world.

I practice this ability and became the best that there is, so I am told.

After being turned my desire to seek revenge on the animals that slaughtered my family seem to all but disappear. For now, I was one and the same an animal who sought sustenance from innocent humans.

243

The Vampire Romance Writer

Finally, after many years my desire to kill those that destroyed my family returned.

I spent many more years hunting each one down and gave them the same treatment that my family received. After I killed all that were involved in my families murders the desire to kill did not end.

I started hunting down humans and killing for the fun of it.

This went on until I met and married Jade, then it only got worse, she loves to hunt and kill humans as much as I did only more.

Jade especially loved to hunt as a couple I did not mind so much either. Jade continued to pull me into the dark side of vampirism, my mother blamed me for the direction Jade, and I was going. Even today, I do not know why Sable did not see the bad side of Jade the side that was darker than I could have ever been.

The Vampire Romance Writer

I think that she felt a connection with her, a motherly connection. Jade was the daughter that she never would have and to this day, she still feels the same about her.

Dillon thoughts were on the wife that Nicholas had where was she now? And what would she do if she knew that he was with an ordinary human woman? Or any woman? Dillon did not want to guess; Dillon voiced her concerns to Nicholas.

Jade would not be happy, she would most certainly try to interfere, try to evoke some type of revenge I am sure, but you don't need to worry I will never let anything happen to you,

I will always be there to protect you.

Dillon pretended that she did not even hear him. I am ready to go back Colorado I need to be getting home I still do not know what to do about you and me. There still is a great deal that I must think about.

245

The Vampire Romance Writer

Nicholas turned her to face him what do you mean? There is not anything to think about, you will be my wife and that will be it.

You can choose anywhere in the world for us to live as long as I am with you, that is all that matters. Money will never be an issue either, so I do not know what there is to think about.

Dillon was not thinking about money, or where they would live. Dillon was not even questioning if she loved him there was no question that she did, and Nicholas knew this.

Dillon was still deciding if wanted this type of life and if she would choose to take it or leave it.

However, for now, Dillon did not want to think about that, she wanted to enjoy this moment, she wanted to enjoy being with him and she knew that he wanted the same thing.

The Vampire Romance Writer

Nicholas pulled her to him taking in her scent then slowly started slipping off each piece of her clothing, with each piece that he removed he slowly kissed the exposed area letting his lips linger on her breasts then slowly down her abdomen as he slid off her jeans and he enjoyed kissing every inch of her.

Her skin seemed to be electrified sending off little sparks of electricity with each kiss.

Nicholas tasted her nectar that flowed from her with his every touch. Even this seemed to be electrified, she tugged at his shoulders beckoning him back up to her, and he willingly obeyed. Dillon drew him to her, both craving each other's kiss and even as their lips touched, each felt as if they would never get their fill.

Nicholas could sense how much she desired him, and he desired her as much maybe more.

What she wanted and needed was for him to fill her with the pleasure that was he and bring her to the point where she almost did not want to return.

The Vampire Romance Writer

Nicholas, he did her bidding and as always took her to a level of sexual pleasure that no man has done before.

Afterward, he held her in his arms until she fell asleep. As Nicholas lay there with Dillon all he could think was how could he have lived all these years without her and having the realization that he was right when he told her before that he could not live without her.

Nicholas stayed there a little longer than he got up and dressed he needed to call and have the plane ready to go, he would let her sleep until they were almost ready to leave.

Nicholas went to speak to Samuel and Sarah to tell them that the plane would be ready soon for their departure.

Nicholas returned to Dillon stood over her and watched her as she lay sleeping.

248

The Vampire Romance Writer

He could see her energy, her heat that still glowed bright white he leaned over her and whispered for her to wake; she slowly opened her eyes smiling up at him.

Oh, how he loved her if she only knew the depth of his love. Dillon slowly touched his face he felt faint but resisted the darkness that wanted to close in around him.

Nicholas wanted to be able to be with her, he could not let himself be consumed by her energy each time she touched him he needed somehow to try to overcome this obstacle.

Dillon wanted to shower before they were to leave, she rose and entered the bathroom gesturing him to follow her, he did as she wished.

As they showered together, once again their desire for each other consumed them until each had diminished their appetite at least for the moment.

The Vampire Romance Writer

Chapter 25

The plane was loaded Dillon and Sarah were on their way back to Colorado each with their own vampire.

Dillon knew that Sarah would be marrying Samuel and most likely have herself changed into a vampire, Dillon though did not know if that was the path that she wanted to take, this was an issue that she would surely have to think over carefully.

Dillon did know that she had fallen madly in love with Nicholas; she may have loved him even before they met.

Dillon knew that Nicholas was the man in her dreams, her nightmares but what she did not understand was how her dreams fit into reality, were they going to come true or was it all in her mind.

250

The Vampire Romance Writer

For the moment Dillon could not focus on her dreams, she had more pressing matters, concerning the here and now.

She had some decisions to be made and some questions to be answered. Dillon had to decide how she was going to live this in this newly discovered world of vampires.

Dillon knew deep down that she could not leave him again. What about the tests what would they show?

Would she be able to continue her contact with him? Was it causing irreparable damage to him? What unseen changes was her touch causing within him? Dillon hoped that she could find the answer to these questions.

When their plane landed back in Colorado Nicholas's driver was waiting. Dillon and Sarah wanted to be dropped off at the cabin Dillon needed to rest and she knew that Nicholas and Samuel needed to replenish their bodies.

The Vampire Romance Writer

They said their goodbyes, but Dillon knew that
Nicholas would not leave her without a guard

of some sort, Dillon did not see anyone or anything
but, she knew that Nicholas would not leave her side
if she were not protected.

Dillon felt completely drained and decided that she
would go straight to bed she left Sarah downstairs
after saying goodnight. As soon as she laid her head
on the pillow Dillon was fast asleep, and her nightmare
began.

The rain was pouring down outside a cold bone-chilling
rain she could feel the cold damp chill pouring in all
around her. Dillon could tell that she was not in the
same familiar hallway this time, but she seemed to be
in what looked like a basement.

The windows all around her were all boarded up and
there seemed to be no way to get out she thought

The Vampire Romance Writer

but how did she get in here? She could not remember.

She could hear the wind howl as it blew through the cracks in the windows, Dillon felt as though the

wind would cut right through her. Dillon could not remember ever being this cold.

Dillon tried to focus her eyes to see the room more clearly, but it was no use.

Suddenly there was a faint light coming from the other side of the room. As her eyes adjusted to this light source Dillon saw a large figure, a man, a very tall husky man but not just any man he was a vampire!

Dillon did not recognize him; he looked as if he could be a bodybuilder and well over six feet tall. You would not want to meet this guy in broad daylight let alone in a dark basement with no way out. Slowly he inched toward her.

The Vampire Romance Writer

However, as he approached her, she did not feel as though he wanted to harm her, closer and closer he got Dillon noticed that his arms were tied behind him and his feet were bound with only enough slack to take small steps.

Dillon knew that she had to try to protect herself even though he was bound. Dillon also knew that vampires were very strong and that she would only have seconds to try to knock him out.

As he stepped closer to her Dillon quickly placed her hands on his shoulders and held them there Suddenly, she saw his eyes roll back and she knew at that moment that he was losing consciousness. Dillon's thoughts were running wild, why would a vampire come so close to her and not even try to run? Or even resist having her touch him?

This vampire must have wanted her to render him unconscious. But why? Dillon kept a tight grip on him. After only a few seconds Dillon released him as

254

the giant vampire fell face down on the floor at her feet.

What followed next happened in a blink of an eye, out of nowhere two other vampires dressed in what seemed like some sort of protective clothing. Each grabbed an arm and held her firmly then a third vampire came face to face with Dillon.

This vampire looked like a goddess, her skin white and smooth her hair jet black and deep-set green eyes.

Dillon had the feeling that compared to her she was no match in beauty, but this was the least of Dillon's worries for the vampire was not here to compare beauty secrets.

When this vampire spoke, it was a cold deep voice the kind that men would find sexy, but Dillon found it very frightening.

So, you are the human that has been sleeping with my husband? How do like being with my husband? Did he tell you that he could not live without you? And that

you were the only women that he has truly thought
that was his soul mate?

Well that is his best line and my dear, here is mine,
the last face that you will see before you die is mine.

Dillon felt a sharp pain in her chest, she looked down
and the vampire had pulled her heart right out of her
chest.

Dillon heard a loud scream like an animal being
slaughtered; the heart-wrenching pain in its voice was
all she could think about just before she died. Dillon
was breathing so fast that she was close to

Hyperventilating she jumped out of bed clenching her
chest, but her legs would not hold her she collapsed
on the floor.

Dillon sat up and leaned against the bed. What had
just happened?

256

The Vampire Romance Writer

Could it have been a vision? Her dreams did seem to be evolving.

Could she really be seeing the future through her dreams?

Whatever it was, it was so real, Dillon had vivid dreams all her life, but she had never had a dream like this one.

Dillon continued to sit there and tried to compose herself, her mind still of her dream, her vision.

There was one thing that Dillon knew for sure, she knew that she had dreamed of Nicholas's ex-wife.

Dillon also knew that if this vampire did not already know of her relationship with Nicholas that it would be only a matter of time until she did.

When she did find out, Dillon knew for certain that she would seek her out, not only for revenge but also to somehow use Dillon's ability to ignite the little bit of life left in vampires.

The Vampire Romance Writer

Dillon finally was able to regain her strength enough
to shower and dress, as she did her mind remained on
her dream, would her dream really come true?

Of course, it would she thought at least some version
of it would and Dillon needed to somehow learn from it
so that it would not end with her death.

Dillon decided that she would tell her dream to
Nicholas as soon as she saw him that evening.

Dillon did not mention her dream to Sarah; Dillon
did not want her to worry Sarah anymore; she had
already put her through enough on this so-called
vacation.

Anyway, Sarah seemed to be enjoying the prospect
of being a vampire and a vampire's wife. Dillon
would, however, have to eventually tell her but just
not yet.

Dillon and Sarah spent the day getting ready to see
their vampires that night being a vampire's girlfriend
258

was not easy on a morning person of which was what they both were.

Both ladies would surely be in need of a nap before their dates that evening. Dillon was not looking forward to sleeping she did not want to be plunged back into her nightmares she did however managed to get a short restful nap in with no interruption from the dream world.

Nicholas knew that something was worrying Dillon as he greeted her that evening. Even though Nicholas could not read her mind or even touch her at this moment, his keen vampire sense in combination with that fact that he knew that she was his soul mate gave him the ability to practically make her thoughts his own.

Dillon took Nicholas aside soon after Nicholas and Samuel had arrived at the cabin that evening and she immediately told him of her dream and her thoughts on it.

Nicholas had to admit that she had described his ex-wife Jade right down to the way her voice seemed to affect males. Nicholas knew that Dillon's dream was indeed a foretelling of the future but in no way was he going to confirm what she already suspected. Nicholas just needed to protect her and find a way to alter the future.

Nicholas tried to reassure Dillon that her dream was just that, a dream.

Nicholas assured Dillon that he would always be there to protect her no mattered what the future would bring. Dillon did not find much comfort in his words of reassurance. Dillon knew all too well that he could not always be there; she also knew that her dreams were trying somehow to warn her of future dangers that lay ahead.

After Dillon told Nicholas of her dream, Nicholas had insisted that the ladies should come and stay with

The Vampire Romance Writer

them; Dillon was not as excited about this suggestion as Sarah was.

Dillon was not as comfortable around all the vampires as Sarah either maybe because Dillon had this gift or curse which one, she had not decided but she knew that this special ability of hers did not make her feel welcome around them.

Dillon felt that either they wanted to gain something from it, or they wanted to harm her because of it. Was this what her dreams and instincts were telling her?

Regardless she guessed that she would be safer around Nicholas, so Dillon agreed to stay there for the time being.

Dillon and Sarah were given rooms next to each other they were at the opposite end of the house from where the vampires' rooms were.

Nicholas thought that this would help ease Dillon's mind but unbeknownst to Nicholas this did very little.

261

The Vampire Romance Writer

Nicholas had also set up for there to be further testing on Dillon. Nicholas's not being able to touch Dillon only after she had deemed him unconscious then reawaken him, was taking a toll on him.

Even though Nicholas felt energized and more powerful after each time Dillon had awakened him and he drank from her, the feeling did eventually diminish leaving him feeling weakened and vulnerable.

Nicholas had promised that he would not let anything happen to her and under normal circumstances, he was a strong, powerful vampire but after an encounter with Dillon, he knew that he was weakened.

It seemed that the only way to keep up that energized feeling that he had after he was intimate with her was to continue to partake of her blood. This was something he was not willing to do; he would not harm her to increase his physical ability.

The Vampire Romance Writer

Nicholas came to the realization that Dillon had another ability to somehow tell the future or at least see parts of it, for her dream, was dead-on concerning the description of Jade.

If Jade knew about Dillon, she would most certainly try to destroy Dillon. Jade still considered him her husband, so Nicholas knew that he had to protect Dillon at all costs.

After Dillon and Sarah settled into their rooms Sarah went down to be with Samuel even though Sarah was not used to the late nights Sarah had no issues with being up most of the night as long as she was with Samuel.

Dillon though could not take the late nights on a steady basis, she did not mind the occasional late night, but this every night thing was getting to her.

Dillon decided not to join them downstairs she felt that she needed to be alone, she wanted to do some research on her computer reading up on all that she

263

The Vampire Romance Writer

could about vampires but still not knowing if what she read was true or not.

After what seemed like hours Dillon gave up her search and went to take a hot bath knowing that Nicholas would be visiting her later, she wanted to be ready when he did.

After her long soak, she returned to her computer to try to search up on anything that would give her insight into what caused her to have the effect that she did on the vampires. Dillon had no idea what she was looking for because up until a few days ago she never even believed that vampires even existed and now they are all around her.

Dillon needed to find out if this power, or whatever it is, does more than resurrect vampires from their day sleep there had to be more to this power.

Dillon tired of her search and decided to lay down but no sooner than she thought this Nicholas was at her

The Vampire Romance Writer

door she knew that he wanted her as much as she wanted him, she was just afraid that she would end up killing him with the slightest touch.

May I come in? Dillon held the door open for him standing clear of him; he was touched by her gesture, knowing that her touch would take him out within seconds.

Hello, my darling how are you this evening? Dillon noticed that he was being standoffish, Dillon could tell that he feared that her dream would come true as much as she did, but he did not want to let on to her that he did.

They sat down on the bed, Dillon being careful not to touch him. Dillon, do you remember anything more about the dream? Dillon told him of the room and of the other vampires, as she did, she watched for any clue that he might recognize anything that she was describing but if he did, he hid it well.

The Vampire Romance Writer

They talked until it was close to dawn, as she walked him to her door, he handed her a key, for later if you need me this is a key to my room.

She took it being careful not to touch him and then he left her to go retire to his bed all alone.

Dillon knew that his giving the key to her was an invitation for her to visit him later and she planned to do just that, but for now, she needed her rest as much as he did, Dillon fell asleep thinking of him.

Around noon Dillon awoke to a knock at her door, she answered, and Sarah was there waiting with lunch for both of them.

Dillon was glad to see Sarah they had gone on this vacation together but had not spent much time together, so it was good to spend a little time with her best friend.

The afternoon was spent just relaxing and discussing what their immediate plans were.

266

The Vampire Romance Writer

Sarah still planned to get to know Samuel better; she was still undecided about what the distant future held for her and Samuel. Prior to sunset Dillon and Sarah agreed that they should get ready for their vampires. Sarah left for her bedroom to get ready for her to meet Samuel later that evening. Dillon decided that before Nicholas woke, she wanted to do a little exploring of this very large house.

Dillon wanted to see if there were any memorabilia from jade lingering in one of these old rooms. Dillon eased down to the library, searching for anything to help her on her quest to find out if her dreams were accurate.

She searched and found nothing but century-old books of every sort, but she found nothing on Vampires and nothing on foretelling the future. Finally, Dillon gave up and returned to her bedroom. Dillon decided to explore another area of the house one where she would definitely find what she was looking for. Dillon headed straight to the bathroom when she got to her room took a quick shower and

The Vampire Romance Writer

applied a little makeup and grabbed the key that was given to her for just this purpose. Dillon was careful not to make too much noise as she crept toward the vampire side of the house, it was getting close to sunset and she still had no idea if all that she had read on the internet about vampires awakening at dusk was true.

Dillon did not want to come face to face with one of the vampires even if Nicholas considered them friendly.

Finally, she made it to Nicholas room without seeing a single being human or vampire.

Dillon eased the key into the lock and pushed one of the heavy doors open the room was dark except for a tiny soft-lit lamp in the corner there was a giant four-poster bed right in the middle of the room that had heavy drapes pulled around it.

The Vampire Romance Writer

Dillon knew that was for his protection there were also large metal blinds that came right out of the walls covering the entire window and completely blocked out the sunlight.

Dillon knew that Nicholas had left the lamp on for her, Vampires could see well with or without light, at least that's what her recent research said.

Dillon slowly walked over to the bed pulled the drapes back just enough, so she could tell where he was, he was laying on the opposite side from where she was standing with his back to her.

Dillon pulled her little vial of smelling salts from her robe then let her robe drop, she stood there completely naked for a few seconds just admiring him before she crawled in beside him.

She gently laid her hand on his bare back, his skin was like ice and just as stiff, this reminded her of why they are called the undead.

269

The Vampire Romance Writer

Nicholas looked and felt just like a person that had been dead for a long time.

Dillon had to push this thought from her mind. Dillon continued to caress his back as she did, she felt him tremble with the touch of her hand, she slowly placed her other hand on his shoulder. Dillon felt him shiver from head to toe as if he was having a seizure.

Oh my God she thought to herself he is having a seizure; Dillon quickly removed her hands this had not happened this violently before.

Dillon waited until the trembling slowed down wondering if she should continue or not.

She decided to continue, she slowly rolled him onto his back uncovered him completely as he lay there, she could not help but think about how beautiful a man he was.

Dillon slowly climbed up onto him with her legs spread open and sat upon his waist and leaned over and
270

began kissing him she felt his skin warm with her every touch.

The trembling returned but she noticed that it was only slight tremors like if you suddenly got a chill.

Dillon took her time enjoying the freedom to do what she wanted to him. His body was responding to her touch, warming with each second that passed.

Dillon kissed his lips softly letting her tongue trace the outline of his lips. Dillon slowly slid her tongue down to his neck running it up and down, feeling him tremble with each lick.

Dillon got the urge to taste him, she started out softly sucking his neck, as she continued, she could taste his blood it had the taste of salt and iron but there was a hint of something else, of which she did not recognize.

As she continued, she could hear Nicholas's voice in her head as if his thoughts were hers, he wanted her to wake him.

271

The Vampire Romance Writer

Dillon let go of his neck and sat up to see if he had spoken to her, but Nicholas was still in his renewal sleep, Dillon knew somehow that his thoughts had entered her mind but how she did not know he had never been able to enter her mind before.

Dillon placed the vial under his nose after he took a couple of shallows breathes, he started to awaken he opened his eyes and once again he grabbed her and began kissing her as if he wanted to devour her.

Nicholas turned to overtake the dominant position and quickly entered her.

Nicholas had the desire to drink from her to taste her; Dillon turned her head to allow him as he kissed her neck. Dillon felt his sharp fangs pierce her neck, and she let out a little moan, which only excited Nicholas even more.

Nicholas continued to drink from her, the heat that emanated from within her started to overwhelm him,

272

The Vampire Romance Writer

the combination of her warmth and her blood was so intense he was sure that he would pass out from sheer pleasure, but he did not, both now were vocalizing the pleasure they were feeling.

The more that Nicholas drank from her the stronger and more alive he felt, as they both climaxed, he released her neck. Nicholas had drunk his fill of her so much so that he could feel the electricity literally flowing through his veins.

He rolled onto his back and pulled her on top of him and she lay there feeling cold and completely drained to the point that she thought that she would pass out.

Nicholas noticed this and quickly placed her on the bed beside him. Nicholas knew that he had drained her not just of her blood but also her warmth and energy. He lifted her head so as to look in her eyes and as he did, they suddenly rolled back into her head and she became lifeless in his arms.

Chapter 26

Nicholas ran down to where Samuel and Sarah were, informed them of Dillon situation when they arrived back to the room Dillon was still unconscious.

Sarah was examining her we need, an ambulance now Sarah shouted, Samuel ran to call the ambulance what happened? Sarah demanded she is frozen, and her heart rate is barely palpable. Nicholas gave her the short and to the point version of their sexual encounter. Sarah had a good idea of the problem not only was she suffering from hypothermia but blood loss .as well.

When the ambulance arrived, Sarah left out the little detail of her being drained of blood she did, however, tell them that she may be anemic at least they would know that she possibly needed blood.

The Vampire Romance Writer

Dillon was transported to the hospital for the second time on her vacation and Nicholas was coming to the conclusion that maybe being around the vampires would end up killing her.

Nicholas arrived at the hospital the same time that the ambulance did, Sarah and Samuel following right behind. When they arrived at the hospital, they would only let Sarah be with Dillon in the exam room, they immediately put a heating blanket on her and started her on warm intravenous fluids.

They were in the process of giving her blood when Dillon woke to the sight of the dark red blood flowing down the IV tubing heading for her vein. Dillon grabbed the IV line and pulled it from her, sending blood pouring onto the floor.

Sarah jumped out of the way of the spewing blood, shouting at Dillon to stop.

I do not want blood Dillon replied, whether you want it or not you need it, or you may die

Dillon remained adamant about this and in the end; she refused to let them give her any blood.

Dillon knew that if she had a blood transfusion, she might never again be able to affect vampires as she now did.

Sarah begged her to reconsider but she remained adamant. Dillon made Sarah promise her to not let anyone, under any circumstances give her no blood or blood products.

Sarah reluctantly agreed and as soon as Sarah agreed, Dillon once again drifted into unconsciousness.

Sarah went to give Nicholas and Samuel an update on Dillon, Nicholas was just as upset as Sarah that Dillon would not accept any blood, he demanded to see her, and after a while, he was finally able to go in and see her.

She was still unconscious, he could sense that she was still very weak, but her warmth had returned he had
276

such a desire to kiss her slowly placed his lips to hers and inhaled her scent, it energized him, his heart filled with love for her.

Nicholas was so concerned over Dillon he was beside himself with worry especially after learning that Dillon refused any type of blood.

Nicholas did not even have to ask Sarah why Dillon did not want the blood. Even if he could not read Sarah's mind, he already knew deep down that
Dillon was afraid of losing whatever this ability of hers if she was given another's blood.

Nicholas stayed in the hospital with Dillon all night just watching her chest slowly rise and fall, worried each time it fell that it might not rise again.

Dillon remained stable that night but still not regaining consciousness, she slept as her dark knight stood watch over her. Nicholas stayed until just before dawn he was replaced by Sarah, knowing that she was safe in Sarah's hands reassured that Sarah would do everything humanly possible to save Dillon.

277

The Vampire Romance Writer

Nicholas left the medical decisions up to Sarah, but he made sure that Dillon life was protected in another way prior to his leaving. Nicholas had set up for Dillon to have not one or two guards but three at her door and one at each of the hospital's entrances. Nicholas had the feeling that Dillon's dream would more than likely come to fruition and he was taking no chances.

Before he left her, he once again kissed her and felt the same energized feeling as before, he whispered softly in her ear that he loved her more than life itself.

As he was leaving, he informed Sarah that he would return at dusk.

Nicholas quickly turned and left his heartfelt as though it would burst from the pain that he felt for leaving her there.

Nicholas reached his house before sunup and spoke with Samuel concerning how the tests were going, thus

The Vampire Romance Writer

far, there was not any compelling evidence explaining why Dillon had the effect that she did on vampires and as for Nicholas's tests, they were more interesting.

It seemed that somehow, he was being revitalized by Dillon's touch. After multiple times enduring her touch and drinking from her, this combination seemed to be regenerating his cells at a fast pace, but further testing would be necessary to determine exactly what this would do to him in the long run.

With this new information Nicholas went to his room and readied himself for bed, he closed his blinds and pulled the drapes around his bed and lay there thinking of her and of the possibility of being somewhat human again...

Nicholas woke feeling better than he could ever remember he quickly jumped out of bed and straight to his shower. Nicholas was dressed within minutes; he did not want to miss a moment of his waking time

The Vampire Romance Writer

without Dillon he needed to get to the hospital and check on her.

His daydreams were, filled with images of her, haunting him in his sleep.

Nicholas flung his bedroom door open and walked straight into a brightly lit hallway.

Nicholas could not understand why there were so many lights on in the house, the house was normally dimly lit but after his eyes had time to adjust to the bright light he was able to focus and see that the light was not coming from any lamps but from the sun! Nicholas immediately dashed back to his room his eyes again adjusting to the change of light and ran to the bathroom to check his body.

Nothing, there was nothing, usually, vampires suffer immediate severe burns and die shortly after the longer the exposure the quicker that they would die but he had been there almost a minute and nothing.

The Vampire Romance Writer

He once again went to his door and this time slowly opened it as he eased out, he was sure that he would burst into flames. Nothing there was nothing, no burning no pain, nothing, he could not believe it.

Yes, he could he thought; he had a feeling all along that Dillon would eventually turn him human again.

Nicholas walked downstairs and straight to the front door he had no doubts concerning Dillon's ability to transform him and he could not resist seeing the sun for the first time in centuries.

As Nicholas opened the door, he felt the warm sun on his face there was no burning only the warm kiss of the sun.

Nicholas had to get to Dillon and tell her of the amazing feat she had accomplished.

Dillon was finally awake and feeling better but weak, Sarah was still at her bedside, you had another, close call, she told Dillon.

It's getting to be a ritual; this is no joking matter Dillon.

You need to be careful we still don't know what we are dealing with, it could be worse next time and you need to remember that the next time something like this happens and let them give you blood, damn you need it now you are still very weak.

I will not take the blood it may alter this ability that I have, and I will not take a chance of losing it.

Even though your life may depend on it. Sarah asked.

Dillon turned over signaling that she was finished with that subject. She would not want to risk losing what she has before she even knew what it was.

Nicholas was so overjoyed to be in the sun after so many years, but he did not waste his time enjoying the sun, right now all he wanted was to get Dillon.

282

The Vampire Romance Writer

Nicholas would have to get used to driving in the daylight he did not even have sunglasses he knew that he would not be able to drive without them.

Nicholas ran back inside to ask Noah if he had any when Noah saw him, he was so surprised that he was speechless.

I don't have time to explain, but sir should we not at least draw some blood samples just to see if there are any metabolic changes.

Nicholas reluctantly agreed, after that, he rushed out with the sunglasses on finding it much better to see with them on.

Nicholas arrived at the hospital within minutes and found Sarah there at Dillon's side with Dillon fast asleep.

How is she doing? Sarah was not surprised to see him with the sun still high in the sky.

The Vampire Romance Writer

Sarah already had the feeling that Dillon's blood was changing him but in what way she did not know.

She updated him on Dillon's condition as he walked to her bedside then Sarah excused herself saying that she would head back to his house.

Nicholas went to her and had no reservations at all about kissing her and that's what he did with no adverse reaction whatsoever. Dillon woke to his kisses and responded to them with full force she also was not surprised to see him in the daylight Dillon greeted him with "welcome back into the sunlight".

I think that maybe you are a new breed of vampire she told him, but he was not interested in that, now.

His concern was for her as he started to scold her on not taking the blood, she touched her finger to his lips to quiet him, listen to me I am fine and that is all that matters not the past, so can we concentrate on our future.

284

The Vampire Romance Writer

Nicholas did not press the issue anymore he decided that it could and be discussed another day, for now, all he wanted was to lay beside her and he crawled in bed with her enjoying being able to touch her at his leisure.

Nicholas stayed with her the rest of that day and all that night.

The next morning before sunup Nicholas left after reassuring Dillon that he would return that afternoon before she was discharged.

He had to make some further testing arrangements before coming to take her home. Sarah would be there around lunchtime to help her prepare to go home.

Nicholas kissed her before he left, he held her in his arms feeling her heartbeat against his chest and feeling his heartbeat a little faster too.

Their kiss did not last long enough for Dillon, but she knew that he did not want to press his luck with the sun just yet, she told him to rest and not worry

285

about her that she would be fine and that she would
see him that afternoon and turned and drifted back
off to sleep after he left.

The Vampire Romance Writer

Chapter 27

Dillon woke feeling extremely groggy and very cold. What had the nurses gave her she wondered and why was it so dark?

The darkness surrounded her; Dillon could not understand why all the lights in the hospital would be out.

Dillon sat up realizing that she was lying on the floor, as she got up, she stumbled then fell back to the floor.

Dillon felt much weaker than she did earlier that day the nurses must have given her another sedative.

Dillon tried again to stand up, this she was able to stand but she still felt dizzy.

Dillon glanced around the room that she was in and saw windows at each end of the long room. Dillon slowly walked to the one closest to her, she noticed that they were boarded up, what was going on? She thought.

Dillon rested her head in her hands trying to clear her head and make the dizziness stop.

Then it hit her, this was what she dreamed about, was this really happening? This could not be. Dillon looked through the boards that barred the window she looked down to the yard below.

All that she could see were trees and the rising sun, other than that she was not able to see anything else.

Dillon made her way to the other window, which was boarded up like the last and out of this one, she could see part of the driveway, Dillon could tell that she had to be in an attic for she was at least four stories up.

Dillon tried her best to see something that might give her a clue as to where she was but all she saw past
288

the driveway were tall mountains in the distance and nothing else.

Dillon inched around the room closing her eyes as she did it seemed to help her concentrate since the room was so dark her eyes only made her mind work harder trying to focus in the pitch black.

Dillon used her sense of touch, which seemed to be magnified when she did not use her eyes; Dillon rubbed her hands along the wall until she found what she was looking for a door!

Dillon turned the handle and of course, it was locked, Dillon banged on the door until her arms no longer had any strength to rise and pound on the door.

Dillon leaned up against the door and slowly slid down onto the floor then let the tears flow.

Nicholas arrived at the hospital just before sunset that evening to find that his guards were nowhere to be found and that Dillon was not in her bed, he went straight to the nursing station to find out where she

The Vampire Romance Writer

was and within a few minutes, he knew that someone
had taken her.

As the hospital staff called for security
Nicholas immediately called Noah and Samuel and
instructed them to meet him at the hospital
immediately. While he waited for their arrival, he had
the security check the cameras and he found what he
was looking for.

He watched as two tall broad-shouldered men dressed
all in black and wearing baseball caps walked up to the
guards that he had stationed there and zapped them
with what must have been stun guns and then dragged
them to another room.

Nicholas watched in horror as the two men then
entered Dillon's room and wheeled her out a few
minutes later.

The Vampire Romance Writer

Nicholas did not get a clear look at their faces, but he did not have to, he already knew that Jade was behind this.

It was Jade, his ex-wife that had kidnapped Dillon.

Nicholas was pretty sure that the two guys were Jade's bodyguards. He could not even begin to think as to where Jade might have taken Dillon.

Samuel and Noah had arrived, and Nicholas filled them in, then he sent Noah to find all that he could find about Jade and where she may have taken Dillon.

Since their divorce, Nicholas had all but forgotten about Jade, now he wished that he would have, at least kept track of her whereabouts.

Nicholas and Samuel headed for his house there was nothing else they could do until they had something to go on and Nicholas would start with his mother.

The Vampire Romance Writer

Dillon sat beside that door for what seemed like hours not knowing what to do, waiting on whoever had brought her here.

Dillon did not need to be told what it was that they wanted that she knew, she also had a pretty good idea as to who was behind this, if her dream was correct and she was sure it was then it would be Jade.

As the thought of Jade was leaving her head, she heard someone coming up the stairs; Dillon jumped up and went to the corner of the room as far away as possible from the door.

The door slowly opened and in walked three vampires one older male and two young female vampires, the male vampire stood guard at the door holding a small dim-lit lamp while the female vampires entered the room.

The Vampire Romance Writer

One of the female vampires was carrying what looked like a change of clothes and a blanket the other was carrying a tray of food and drinks.

Dillon tried to keep her eyes on all three at the same time. Dillon watched as the vampires sat the items on the floor in the middle of the room then walked out of the room without saying a word. The male vampire then placed the lamp on the floor just inside the door then quickly closed and locked the door behind him.

After they left Dillon did not care about the food, but she wanted to get out of the hospital gown, she changed quickly then wrapped herself in the blanket, walked over and sat by the window willing Nicholas to hear her thoughts.

Nicholas sat in the passenger's seat as Samuel drove towards Nicholas's house, Nicholas was lost in his thoughts when Dillon's voice entered his head, she was trying to tell him that she was alright and tell him all that she could about who had her and where she was.

But how could this be? Nicholas thought Nicholas had never been able to read her thoughts before, but he was not reading her mind, no, she was somehow communicating with him telepathically.

Dillon told him that she was fine for the moment and that he was right about Jade wanting to seek revenge on her.

Jade had her locked up in what must be an attic but as to where she was, she did not know.

Dillon informed him that there were at least three vampires there; two young female vampires and a slightly older male vampire.

Dillon further showed him images of the landscape surrounding where she was being held showing him what she saw when she looked out the windows. Nicholas saw the mountains that she had seen, and he saw the trees and driveway that she had also seen.

The Vampire Romance Writer

If he could locate the mountains that she showed him, then he could find her.

Dillon repeated over and over that she loved him and that she knew that he would find her and that she did not doubt his love for her before fading from his mind.

Nicholas's anger was building up inside knowing that Jade was truly behind her abduction; Jade had better not let him find her, he would surely kill Jade when he did.

Dillon fell asleep by the window when she woke, she had the feeling that her attempt to give Nicholas a message worked she did not know how she knew but somehow, she just knew it did. Dillon felt it deep down inside, she also felt his love for her and the anger that was raging inside of him for Jade.

Dillon had a feeling that it would not end well for Jade if Nicholas found her.

Dillon sat there until what seemed like the early morning hours, she heard nothing more from the

The Vampire Romance Writer

vampires and unable to hold her eyes open any longer she drifted off into a restless sleep.

It seemed like she had only been asleep a short while when Dillon woke to find someone was injecting her with what she thought could be another sedative.

As Dillon drifted in and out of consciousness, she could tell that she was being moved to another room by two vampires wearing some type of suits that seemed to be made of rubber.

Dillon was moved to what looked like a very large bathroom with, what also appeared to and examination table right in the middle of the room.

They laid her on the table, then straps were placed on her arms and legs and across her forehead. Then more straps were wrapped around her wrists and pulled tight, this process was repeated with her ankles.

One of the female vampires came and injected her with another sedative, as Dillon fought to stay awake

The Vampire Romance Writer

she watched as one of the vampires withdrew blood from her but instead of it being placed in a vial it was placed in a wine glass and given to who she knew was Jade!

Dillon watched as Jade drank her blood still fighting to remain conscious, but her fight was fruitless the sedative finally overtook her.

While Dillon lay unconscious Jade finished drinking the rest of Dillon's fresh drawn blood as she did Jade started to feel as though her whole insides were on fire the sensation was like having boiling hot blood to flow through her veins.

Jade dropped to her knees unable to stand due to the pain that was overtaking her. Her fellow vampires ran to try to help but Jade shouted no one is to touch me, she ordered.

Jade continued to feel what she knew was Dillon's blood circulating through her bloodstream, it made her feel stronger and her senses also seemed magnified; it

297

was as if Dillon's blood had somehow amplified her vampire abilities.

All vampires were strong but with Dillon's blood in her Jade felt ten times stronger.

She did not remember ever feeling this good. After finally recovering from the initial shock of Dillon's blood to her system, Jade was able to compose herself and pick herself up off the floor and returned to where she was sitting.

Not saying a word to no one, she sat there and thought to herself she had found the reason that Nicholas wants to keep this human close to him.

Jade ordered that more blood be taken from Dillon, Jade also wanted to do a little experiment, she wanted to see what would happen when a vampire came in contact with Dillon flesh.

First Jade had one of the young female vampire's touch Dillon's arms slightly, as soon as the vampire

298

touched Dillon she immediately fell to the floor, take
her out of here! Jade ordered. Jade walked over to
Dillon, stood there over her thinking what it could be
that she has in her blood that would take down a
vampire with just the slightest touch.

Jades plan had always been to kill Dillon but now she
would let her live, long enough at least to find out
the secret that her touch and blood held, then she
would drain her of all her blood and sit there and wait
to hear the last beat of her human heart.

Jade would enjoy seeing the pain on Nicholas's face
when he found out his precious Dillon was no more.

Jade took the glass of Dillon's blood and left the
room thinking that she would enjoy the literal
lifeblood of her husband's mistress as
Dillon lay strapped down like a wild animal.

Chapter 28

Nicholas had that one telepathic message from Dillon and then nothing and he still no idea as to where she was. Nicholas still had the feeling that his mother held the key to where he might find Jade; he knew that if anyone could lead him to jade it would be his mother.

When Nicholas arrived back at his house he found his mother sitting in his study, Nicholas did not need to try to read his mother's mind the look on her face told him that she knew where Dillon might be but more than that, he knew that she had been the one to give Dillon to Jade!

Mother, what have you done? Sable sat there and said nothing just a blank stare on her face when she finally spoke, she did so in such a low tone that would have been inaudible for a human to hear.

The Vampire Romance Writer

What I did, I did for your own good she was slowly killing you, with her every touch and with each drop of her blood.

Each time you had any contact with her you were becoming more and more human again and thus when you are fully transformed, I will cease to have a son and you will die as all mortals do a broken old man.

Nicholas's anger was building up inside of him he knew that he would soon lose control and he would not be able to stop himself. Where is Dillon mother? Was all that he was able to say, anything more and he knew that the beast that lay deep within him would not stop until it killed its prey, his own mother.

I could not let her destroy you, Nicholas, you must understand what she is capable of, I have known her kind for many centuries and they were put on this earth to transform our kind back to human.

Nicholas's anger was starting to subside; He stood listening to his mother's every word.

The Vampire Romance Writer

Sable had the information that they sought all along, she knew the answers that they were seeking, and she withheld them.

Nicholas had to control his raging anger long enough to find the answers that he needed, to understand what exactly Dillon was.

She would tell him what he wanted to know then he would make her tell him where Dillon was.

Tell me mother all that you know about Dillon, he sat by the fireplace not wanting to be too close to his mother fearing that he would most certainly lose control.

I know that her kind can transform vampires back to human and that as long as there have been vampires there have been what our ancestors called "The Fire Angels", the first ones were placed in the wombs of vampires and as they grew in the vampire's womb they transformed their surrogate mother back to human.

302

When the Fire Angel baby was born it was blessed with some of the powers of its vampire mother in addition to the power to turn any vampire back to human with the both her blood and her touch.

They can transform with the two different ways because if there was a vampire strong enough to withstand her touch and then drank her blood he would still be turned back into a human.

As for Dillon, she is not like any of the Fire Angels that I have known or heard of.

She is different, how exactly I could not say but she seems stronger in some ways weaker in others.

Dillon's touch is the most powerful that I have ever seen, to render a vampire unconscious with just her touch but not immediately transform them this is most unusual.

As for her blood, it is completely different it shows no signs of the power of the Fire Angel on a microscopic level, as had other Fire Angels.

The Vampire Romance Writer

Dillon seems to be a different type of Fire Angel, a more powerful upgraded version.

Not only does she differ in these areas there is one other difference that I have taken note of, no one can read her thoughts unless she wants you to, with all the other Fire Angels we could read their thoughts with ease.

That is why she is so dangerous to vampires you would never know what she is if she did not want you to know.

Nicholas are you so blinded by this woman that you do not know what she can do to you.

She must be destroyed before she learns what she truly is and uses her power to destroy the entire vampire race.

No sooner had his mother had finished her last word, when Nicholas had sped to her and pulled her from her seat, slammed her against the wall, tell me where

304

she is mother? Or I will kill you myself, this is my soul mate, my future wife that you are talking about destroying, now tell me where she or I will destroy you.

Nicholas did not notice that his father and Samuel had entered the room.

Erick and Samuel went immediately on either side of Sable and Nicholas trying to get Nicholas to let go of her, Erick tried to get Nicholas to release Sable, son listen, let her go we will find Dillon, killing your mother will do no one any good.

Tell me mother, where is she? He loosened his grip on her neck just enough to allow her to speak.

Tell him! Erick told his wife, tell him now! Sable knew that she would have to tell him, or she would lose him forever, son please forgive me, I was only looking out for you, mother I don't need anyone to look out for me, where is she?

Sable finally gave in to her son, Jade has taken her to her home just northwest of Aspen, she gave him the address and within seconds, he was on his way with Samuel and Erick following right behind.

The Vampire Romance Writer

Chapter 29

Dillon felt herself slipping away, she knew that if she was drained of any more blood, she would not last the night, she had had been removed from the table and was back in the attic. Dillon lay there fighting to stay conscious, fighting to stay alive.

Even though he was driving at top speed Nicholas was not getting to Dillon fast enough, the rain was pouring down making it the driving treacherous, but he knew that if he did not get to Dillon soon that it would be too late.

Nicholas knew that Jade would waste no time killing Dillon as soon as she had gotten what she wanted from her, at this moment, he had no care for his own life or anyone else's except Dillon's. Nicholas knew that Jade would have the place heavily guarded, but he did not care he
would fight to the death for her.

The Vampire Romance Writer

When he arrived at Jade's home Nicholas did not stop
for the gate, he hit the gate with such force that it
flew completely off crashing yards away into the
garden, he then drove straight into the house,
bursting through the front doors.

Before Nicholas could get out of his car, he was
surrounded by three vampires, a large vampire that
was at least a foot taller than Nicholas came at him
first. He threw Nicholas against a stone wall but that
did not faze Nicholas, he got up, ran toward him, and
tore into his chest ripping his heart out.

The other two vampires each grabbed one of Nicholas's
arms and were trying to bring him to his knees.

Nicholas was able to fling one completely across the
room, then took the other by his head and slung him
around hitting his body against the wall, Nicholas
watched as the vampire's body flew across the floor,
leaving Nicholas holding his head in his hands.

The Vampire Romance Writer

Nicholas dropped the vampires head and ran toward the attic; he was running so fast, all that could be seen was a blur.

Nicholas knew that this was where Dillon was being held, this was her dream truly coming to life.

When Nicholas reached the third level, there were two more vampires there the first one grabbed Nicholas by the neck trying to rip his head off but within seconds, the vampire fell to the floor unconscious.

The other vampire took notice of this and tried to run away from Nicholas, but Nicholas caught him ripped his fangs into his throat-ripping his head off in the process.

Nicholas realized that his drinking of Dillon's blood combined with her touch had not only increased his vampire strength but also gave him the ability to also bring down other vampires with his touch, although not as easily as Dillon but there was no doubt that he could.

The Vampire Romance Writer

His new ability must show itself when the adrenaline was at a heightened level in his body.

There was no denying that he had been changed in many ways by Dillon; she had not changed him back to human, but she had sure changed him.

Nicholas continued to make his way toward Dillon, he was met with two more vampires this time it was the two young female vampires and like the other two, they were out with just the touch of his hands.

Nicholas finally reached the attic door bursting through he found Dillon lying there lifeless on the floor.

Nicholas bent down and lifted her into his arms he could still feel life in her, but it was fading fast.

As he turned to leave, he was met at the door by

310

Jade! Nicholas held Dillon in one arm and grabbed Jade with the other, but she did not drop like the rest, her ability to withstand his touch was evident but her strength was no match for his.

Nicholas shoved her through the door and over the railing, he continued down the hall where he was met by three more vampires standing blocking his way to the stairs.

Nicholas would have to leave Dillon for the moment, he decided to place her back in the room where she had been held.

Nicholas ran full speed at the three vampires hitting them so hard that they all four bursts through the wall out into the stormy night.

Dillon tried to will herself to stand, it took her a few tries, but she finally was able to stand, Dillon, walked slowly toward the door and in the direction that Nicholas had run.

The Vampire Romance Writer

It seemed to Dillon that she was moving in slow motion, but she knew that each step she got closer and closer to the staircase and to Nicholas.

As Dillon walked down the long hall, she glanced out the hall windows she could see that it storming outside. The rain seemed to be blowing sideways and she jumped with each clap of thunder the sound reminded her of a gunshot.

Dillon continued but the closer she got to the staircase she noticed that one corner of the house was gone. Dillon quickly realized that she was living her dream, her nightmare.

Dillon immediately started backing up toward the attic door, Dillon was focused on the damaged wall that she did not notice that Jade was right behind her holding a large metal staff.

The Vampire Romance Writer

Jade raised the staff high in the air then lowered it hitting Dillon on the head and slamming her into the wall.

Dillon lay there barely conscious with what little blood she had left spilling onto the floor. Dillon managed to open her eyes as Jade pulled a long blade from the top of the staff, raised it above
Dillon's heart, suddenly there was a scream Noooo!

Dillon watched as Jade turned her head in the direction of the staircase, Dillon let her eyes follow in the same direction.

Even with blood pooling in her eyes, Dillon was able to see enough to tell that the scream came from Nicholas just before the darkness closed in around her.

Erick and Samuel had arrived as Nicholas and the other vampires came bursting out the corner of the house, each one started battling a vampire.

The Vampire Romance Writer

After Nicholas had destroyed the vampire that he was battling he leaped back up to where Dillon was and saw as Jade was about to stab her with her blade he screamed as Dillon passed out.

Nicholas ran as fast as the lightning that was still striking outside, he reached Jade just before the blade reached Dillon's chest.

Nicholas hit Jade full force sending them both back into the attic. Jade was able to escape his grasp and headed toward the window, but Nicholas was right behind her and again hit her with such force that they two went straight through the wall.

They landed on the rain-soaked ground below, Nicholas trying hard to destroy his ex-wife for trying to kill his soul mate, but she was strong, stronger than ever before. Nicholas realized that Jade had been ingesting Dillon's blood for the powers it held.

314

The Vampire Romance Writer

Jade sent Nicholas flying off her and into the trees where he landed a few yards away.

Jade was there beside him within seconds, Nicholas was ready for her as she came at him, he was prepared to tear through her chest and rip her blacked heart out.

However, she was able to move out of the way before his hand could even touch her. Jade ran toward the forest that lined her property Nicholas caught her by her neck swung her around and bit into her neck with his fangs. As her blood started to pour out, he noticed that it was not dark brownish red like other vampires but a bright red this was the final clue to his belief that she was also being transformed in some way by Dillon's blood.

His bite wounded Jade but she was still strong and tried to use her fangs to bite into Nicholas's throat, but she was unable. Nicholas took her by her hair and sent her flying into a nearby tree, Nicholas could hear her bones breaking as she hit the tree. Nicholas

315

The Vampire Romance Writer

walked toward Jade to finish what he had come here to do but in an instant, his mother was there blocking his way.

No, Nicholas, you have gone too far I will not let you destroy your own wife; Jade took the chance that was given to her and flew off into the tree line and into the darkness.

Nicholas tried to go after her, but Sable blocked his way once again this time he pushed her out of his way but by then Jade was long gone.

His anger was now focused on his mother Nicholas walked up to her to take his anger out on her, but Samuel urgently called for him, Dillon needs you now; this matter between you and your mother and Jade can wait.

Nicholas ran to Dillon's side, Dillon lay there lifeless, we must get her to my house Nicholas said aloud not really speaking to anyone; Erick had the car waiting.

316

The Vampire Romance Writer

Samuel drove while Nicholas cradled Dillon in the back seat.

When they arrived back to Nicholas's house, Nicholas took Dillon straight to his room and laid her gently on his bed.

I will need some equipment I am going to transfuse her with my own blood; Nicholas knew that this would be the only way to save her.

Nicholas had Samuel withdraw two bags of blood from him and immediately hung them and had them infusing slowly into her veins within minutes, he also gave her IV fluids to help with the dehydration, she most certainly had from nearly been drained of all her blood.

Nicholas lay beside her after all the blood and fluids had infused knowing that he had done all that he could do.

The Vampire Romance Writer

The sun was just beginning to rise when he had the blinds and curtains pulled around them, he would rest with her in his arms.

Dillon woke to a dark room she still felt weak but rejuvenated she had no idea as to where she was, she felt around the bed that she was on and found Nicholas lying there beside her.

Dillon knew then that Nicholas had rescued her and brought her back here to his home, his bed.

The Vampire Romance Writer

Chapter 30

Dillon eased out of the bed pulling the bed curtains
closed behind her. Dillon went to his bathroom to
shower, cleansing herself of the dried blood that
covered her, then ran the tub full of hot water and
soaked there letting the hot water soothe her muscles.

Dillon reluctantly pulled herself from the tub,
dried off, and then went to him wearing not
even a towel. Dillon pulled the curtains back
crawled upon him began kissing every inch of
him, ending at his lips but to her surprise, he
returned her kisses.

Nicholas sat up in bed leaned against the
headboard pulled her to him, her legs opened,
she placed one on each side of him giving him
permission to enter at his will.

319

The Vampire Romance Writer

As he kissed her, he cupped her breasts in his hands,
then moved his hands slowly behind her gripping her
bottom, lifting her onto him.

Dillon felt so much pleasure when he entered her that
she moaned, a moan that showed him the satisfaction
and pleasure that he gave her.

Nicholas's lips moved from hers, past her neck to one
breast then the other.

Her body was like fire she burned him inside and out,
as her heat mixed with his icy touch it made their
union much more intense, suddenly he could read her
every thought, they were as one.

Her pleasure was building in sync with his and they
both experienced a climatic pleasure that neither one
of them had experienced before.

320

The Vampire Romance Writer

Afterward, she lay there on top of him, she fell asleep with his arms wrapped around her feeling there was not another place in this world that she would rather be.

Nicholas lay there while she slept thinking of how much he loved her, and that he would never let any harm come to her. Dillon was his soul mate and she would be his wife forever.

Dillon woke exactly where she had fallen asleep, lying there on Nicholas's chest.

He was just lying there watching her, I love you was the first words he told her, and I love you she replied.

They showered and dressed then went downstairs to meet with Samuel and Sarah.

They found Sarah and Samuel down in the study that evening, Sarah had decided to marry Samuel and he would transform her in time.

The Vampire Romance Writer

Dillon and Nicholas congratulated them; Dillon told Sarah that she thought that was the best decision that she could have made.

Dillon reached for Nicholas 's hand and led him outside under the gazebo where a cold gentle rain was falling.

I had given up on ever loving anyone again, I had decided to spend my final years on this earth alone, but now that I have found you, I cannot imagine ever being without you.

You have always been inside me, here in my heart, I have been searching for you, searching all these centuries for my soul mate and I have finally found her, and I will never let you go.

You and I were always meant to be together; we just did not know it until now.

Dillon wrapped her arms around his neck and pulled herself up to kiss him, and whispered, you have
322

searched and now you have found me I am going nowhere, I am your Fire and you are my Ice and I will be yours for eternity.

THE END...

The Vampire Romance Writer

Frozen Flames

The fresh layer of ice on the tree branches swaying in the wind was all that could be heard as she walked down the narrow dirt road that led deep into the mountains, this road was familiar to her but still, she did not recognize where she was.

As she continued up the road and deeper into the mountains, she heard voices, faint but voices no less she could not imagine who else would be out on a cold night like this. She walked on closer and closer toward the voices then a blood-curdling scream stopped her in her tracks, suddenly she felt a cold sensation rising from her feet and the coldness climbed quickly up her entire body leaving her frozen.

Dillon awoke, feeling the cold that had left her frozen in her dream, as she lay there trying to shake off the bad feeling that her dream had left lingering in her. She could not stop wondering where Nicholas might be, she knew he would not stop until he found her, but she also knew that if she stayed with him, his life dead or not would end forever.

The Vampire Romance Writer

About the Author

Connie Ruth Vejar is a native of eastern Kentucky and

has resided most of her adult life in central Florida.

Her passion is writing Vampire Romance Novels.

Vampire Romance Writer

Vampire Romance Writer

Author of Fire and Ice, Frozen Flames and many more
Vampire Romance Novels just waiting to be written.

Made in the USA
Monee, IL
24 October 2021